"You married a man old enough to be your father!"

The look in his eyes mirrored the contempt in his voice. "And, you have to admit, you gave a good impression of enjoying life as the vacuous sex-object wife."

"Age has nothing to do with love," she argued. "And I wasn't vacuous. I was shy, tongue-tied..."

"Oh, come now," he scorned. "Shy? Tongue-tied?"

"Yes," she insisted. "At first."

"Well, you soon learned what was expected of you. I've never seen such an accomplished courtesan, dripping all over your escort, eating him up with your eyes, laughing deliciously at every joke he made. And the clothes you wore. Or *didn't* wear, more accurately. Hardly the way a *shy* woman would dress."

MIRANDA LEE was born and brought up in New South Wales, Australia. She had a brief career as cellist in an orchestra, and then another as a computer programmer. A move to the country after marriage and the birth of the first of three daughters limited her career opportunities to being a full-time wife and mother. Encouraged by her family, she began writing in 1982. She favors a well-paced what-happens-next kind of story, but says what matters most "is that my books please and entertain my readers, leaving them feeling good and optimistic about love and marriage in our present topsy-turvy world."

Books by Miranda Lee

MIRANDA LEE

A Date With Destiny

Harlequin Books

TORONTO • NEW YORK • LONDON
AMSTERDAM • PARIS • SYDNEY • HAMBURG
STOCKHOLM • ATHENS • TOKYO • MILAN
MADRID • WARSAW • BUDAPEST • AUCKLAND

ISBN 0-373-11651-9

A DATE WITH DESTINY

CHAPTER ONE

'Do come in, Mrs Diamond.'

Salome gave the man still seated behind the desk a cool look.

'You're very punctual,' he added with a cursory glance at his watch.

'Ralph was not one of those men who liked to be kept waiting,' she said, before realising that she was talking about her husband in the past tense.

But then came the bitter reminder that, for *her*, Ralph Diamond *was* past. Otherwise Charles Smeaton, Ralph's long-time legal adviser, would have been on his feet, extending a polite hand and showing a wide smile beneath his pencil-thin moustache. Instead, he waved curtly towards the vacant chair in front of the desk.

Salome closed the door of the office far more politely than her inner turmoil warranted. She walked across the plushly carpeted floor, well aware that Charles's beady eyes were running over her eye-catching figure with an insolence he would never have dared display in front of Ralph.

But she sat down and crossed her long, shapely legs without batting an eyelid. If there was one thing her husband had taught her, it was to show apparent indifference to what others did or said.

'You will have to learn to ignore the gossip, Salome,' Ralph had warned her right from the start. 'There's bound to be plenty, with your being only nineteen to my forty-nine. People who don't know you will think you're marrying me for my money, in exchange for which I get to bed the most beautiful girl God ever put breath into. There's no point in telling the world the truth, my dear. No one will believe you. You'll just have to learn to live with the slurs. But don't worry, I'll teach you how to distance yourself from malicious tongues, how to hold yourself above them.'

Ralph had been right, of course. People *had* thought the worst of her. Not that they had ever shown their true faces in front of her husband. He was too rich and powerful to offend directly. But there'd been looks and sniggers behind his back. Once, shortly after their marriage, Charles had cornered her at a party and told her to make hay while the sun shone, since dear old Ralph had a habit of discarding his material possessions with regular monotony.

For ages afterwards Salome had been plagued with doubts about the sincerity of Ralph's love. But as the months passed—very happy months— she had gained more and more confidence in herself and her unusual marriage. The doubts were firmly buried, and remained so for over four years, only to resurface with a vengeance one day in May last year—the day Ralph had told her their marriage was over.

'Well, Charles?' she asked, setting cool green eyes upon his smarmy-looking expression. 'Why did you want to see me? I received the final divorce papers in the mail last week. What more is there to be said?'

'You're looking as ravishing as ever, Mrs Diamond,' he drawled, leaning his fleshy frame back into the swivel-chair and giving her the benefit of a further scrutiny, this time letting his eyes linger more insultingly on the thrust of her high, well-rounded breasts.

Salome didn't flinch an inch.

'It's Miss Twynan now, Charles,' she said with silky smoothness. 'Or Salome, if you prefer.' The sudden thought that her ex-husband would have been proud of her unruffled demeanour only brought pain. Oh, Ralph...why did you do it? Why marry me, make my whole life revolve around you, then toss me out like a worn-out shoe? *Why?*

An ugly smile twisted the lawyer's thick lips. 'Salome. Such an...*interesting* name.'

'Molly liked it.'

'Molly?'

'My mother.'

'Ah, yes...your mother.' His derisive tone suggested that just mentioning her mother was distasteful.

'Couldn't we get to the point, Charles?' she asked icily.

He snapped forward on the chair, reefed open a drawer on his left, and extracted a set of keys. 'Ralph has decided to add another item to your settlement,' he announced, tossing the keys forward to land on the edge of the desk nearest Salome. 'A penthouse unit at McMahon's Point. And you'll find the white Ferrari he gave you for your twenty-first birthday in the basement car park.' He leaned back again and gave her another one of those smirky smiles. 'Why you left it behind in the first place, I have no idea. It wasn't as though you didn't *earn* everything Ralph gave you. He always seemed very satisfied with you during your—er—marriage.'

Salome's chest squeezed so tight with the effort to remain composed that she could scarcely breathe.

'I don't want them,' she managed to get out.

'Too bad. The unit has already been transferred into your name by deed gift, and the car was always legally yours. It's registered in your name.'

Salome took a deep breath. No way did she want to stay here arguing with this ghastly man. She would just take the unit and the car, sell them, then give the money to charity, as she had all the other money Ralph had settled on her. For how could she ever keep any of it? To do so would vindicate all the implied insults she'd endured over the years.

Not that any of her slanderers knew about her Grand Gesture. Nor Charles for that matter. She saw little point in telling people like him about something they couldn't possibly understand. They wouldn't appreciate her motives. They would think her crazy. Her own *mother* had thought her crazy!

'Why is he giving me this penthouse now?' she asked. 'Do you know? Did he say?'

Charles shrugged. 'You know Ralph. He never explains his actions. He just gives orders.'

Yes, she thought ruefully. That was Ralph all over.

'We'll go here tonight, Salome,' he would say. 'Order the prawn dish, Salome' or 'Wear the green dress, Salome.'

Most women would have hated his autocratic, bossy nature. But, for reasons which she had not explored deeply enough at the time, Salome had loved it. She had had many long, lonely nights since then to work out why she had acted so submissively. And, while she could appreciate the reasons behind her behaviour, she still wasn't all that comfortable with it.

'I see,' she said tautly. 'Have you got an address for this unit? McMahon's Point is just north of the Harbour Bridge, on the Luna Park side, isn't it?'

'That's right. Yours is penthouse two, in a multi-storeyed circular block called Harbourside Towers, right on the water at the end of Harbour Road. You can't miss it. I—er—presume you'll be moving in right away? After all, you can't really be liking living with your mother.'

Salome picked up the keys and slipped them into her handbag. 'You're quite wrong, Charles,' she said coolly. 'I won't be moving in, and I quite like living with my mother.' But only since Molly seemed finally to have got over the urge to ask every man she dated to move in with her, Salome thought wearily.

She stood up, automatically smoothing down the emerald-green wool sheath over her slender thighs, then, with her free hand, flicking the long mass of tight coppery curls back from her face and shoulders.

A dry-mouthed shock took hold of her when she became aware of how openly lustful Charles's gaze had grown as it followed each of these movements. Her eyes locked on to his with a sickening jolt inside, but she glared back at him quite boldly, till he was forced to drop his eyes.

Creep! she thought savagely.

'Please don't bother to show me out,' she said, making no attempt to hide her sarcasm. And with that she turned on her black high heels and strode from the office.

It wasn't till she was alone in the elevator that she realised she was shaking with fury.

Salome walked slowly through the penthouse, her emotions no more settled than when she had left Charles's office. Her troubled gaze travelled around the enormous living-room she was standing in, taking in the no-expense-spared décor: the classically neutral colour scheme, the ultra-modern imported furniture, the huge, semicircular plate-glass windows that she'd discovered slid back electronically to allow access to the equally huge balcony.

She wandered out to lean on the high cylindrical railing, and frowned at the view, which stretched across to Darling Harbour on her right, Milson's Point on her left, and the Bridge straight ahead. The blue waters were cold-looking but beautiful beneath the clear winter sky. A crisp breeze ruffled Salome's hair, making her realise how cool and refreshing this balcony would be in the summer.

How much was this place worth? she wondered. A million dollars? More?

She sighed. Molly was going to go off her brain when she told her she was going to give it all away too. Just as well Ralph had seen fit to give his young bride's not-so-suitable mother a house and income of her own when they got married, or she'd never hear the end of it. As it was, Molly often brought up the matter of money and how stupid Salome had been to give it all away, then have to go and work in a dress shop to earn her own living.

Which reminded her. She had still not told Molly that it looked as if she was going to be laid off soon. Sales at the boutique were slumping, along with the economy, the manager not minding at all that Salome had asked for the afternoon off. She'd been looking around for a better job but had found she wasn't qualified for anything that paid well. To go back to waitressing was too depressing a thought to consider, but she might have to do just that while going to tech and getting herself some marketable skills. Perhaps a typing and word-processing course. That seemed very much in demand.

Meanwhile she would have to face her mother's exasperation.

Perhaps she wouldn't tell Molly about this unit at all, Salome mused. Perhaps she would only mention the car. She couldn't get out of telling her about that, since she had already decided to drive the Ferrari back to her mother's place at

Killara that afternoon, then take it to one of the luxury-car dealers the next morning. There were a lot along the Pacific Highway up towards Hornsby.

But she really *wanted* to talk to someone about Ralph, wanted a sounding-board for the agony of frustration that she felt building up again inside her. A string of whys had been whirling in her head for too long a time, and now she had another to add to the list. Why had he given her this unit?

But her main questions dealt with the past. Why had Ralph cut her out of his life so abruptly and cruelly? And why, in the light of what had happened, had he married her in the first place? For, to have done what he ultimately had, he couldn't possibly have loved her, as he'd claimed to.

Salome groaned at the crazed complexity of it all. If sex had been involved it might have made some sense! She was used to men claiming they were in love with a woman till they were firmly ensconced in her bed, only to desert her several months later when their lust had begun to pall. She'd watched them do it to Molly for years!

But her relationship with Ralph had not been a physical one, so sexual boredom—or another woman—could not be blamed for Ralph's divorcing her.

Suddenly, Salome's chest contracted viciously, seized by a defiant surge of anger. This was the overriding emotion she was experiencing lately. Anger. A bitter, frustrated anger.

'*Why?*' she screamed out across the water.
'*Why?*'

It felt oddly good to give voice to her pain,
even if only to empty air. In fourteen long
months, Salome had been denied the outlet of
actually screaming at Ralph, for he refused to see
her, refused to let her get past the blanket of security he had wrapped himself in.

He had moved to his rural property out at
Dural, on the outskirts of Sydney, his enormous
mansion in Potts Point having been sold within
weeks of their separation taking effect. Salome
had driven out to Dural several times in vain at-
tempts to gain entrance to see Ralph. But to no
avail.

Her letters were returned unopened.

As for phone calls ... Valerie always answered
the telephone, and there was no denting Ralph's
secretary's relentlessly negative stance. Not that
the woman was rude. She was just totally im-
movable. Ralph had given orders that his ex-wife
was not to be put through to him, and that was
that!

Every which way Salome turned, her path was
blocked. Finally she had been forced to give up,
and had been trying to make a new life for herself.
But it hadn't been easy. Not easy at all.

Today she had put on a brave front for Charles,
but inside she was still a shattered woman, a
woman who had married for love, not money, a
woman who had never been the cheap, mercenary, gold-digging little tart others had always
believed her to be.

Though you have to admit, Salome, she conceded to herself with a certain irony, you can't really blame people for thinking that was the case. You *were* thirty years younger than Ralph and—my God—the nineteen-year-old Salome Twynan would have made Eliza Doolittle look classy!

Salome ran an agitated hand through her windblown hair. If she impressed people now as a well-groomed, sophisticated and articulate lady then it was Ralph Diamond who was responsible for that. Ralph, who had shown her how to walk and talk and dress and act; Ralph, who had educated her in matters of manners and music and, yes, even men, to a degree.

As the wife of a successful businessman she'd been required to do a lot of entertaining, mostly in male company. Ralph had shown her how to be the perfect hostess to his male guests, which included knowing exactly what role to play to charm their particular personalities. Sometimes she was an intent listener, at others a witty conversationalist. Above all, she was always required to look as beautiful as possible.

This miracle had not been achieved overnight. It had taken time, but Ralph had eventually remade the rough Mrs Diamond into a sparkling jewel, coated with a polish, the veneer of which not even his abandonment had destroyed.

Oh, Ralph! Salome groaned. Why? Was I ever anything more to you than just another possession, to be toyed with for a while, then discarded when the game tired you? Have you found some other naïve, innocent young thing to make over to your requirements? Was that the object of it all? Do you get your kicks out of playing God with other people's lives?

Tears welled up into her eyes. She turned and walked slowly back inside, unconcerned when the tears began to overflow and run down her cheeks. What did it matter? A good cry was what she needed. She sank down on to one of the plush leather sofas, her head dropping into her hands.

A loud, rapid knocking on the door gave her an awful fright.

Her head jerked up, her fingers moving in a frantic attempt to dry her cheeks. She blinked rapidly with some success, and began moving towards the door, automatically tidying her messy hair with her hands. Who on earth could it be? Her stomach twisted with a rush of nerves at having to ward off someone awkward. Like Charles.

But then she thought of the building's security system, and relaxed. She had had to give the uniformed guard in the foyer a list of the people she would allow to come up without checking first with her. And she had only given her mother's name.

Yet her mother didn't even know about this place yet. Salome frowned. She had come here straight from Charles's office. Slipping the safety-chain into place, she slowly opened the door. 'Who is it? Who's there?' she asked sharply, worried when the small gap didn't reveal any part of a human being.

A man moved into the space, a man whose cleft chin rested at her eye level. She looked up and saw the blackest of black eyes peering at her from beneath equally black brows and hair. Then realised they all belonged to a person she actually knew. 'Good heavens!' she exclaimed, startled.

The object of her shock said nothing for a moment, a fierce frown gathering his straight brows together as he stared at her through the narrow slit.

Finally he spoke. '*Mrs* Diamond?' There was puzzlement—and a definite hint of antag-onism—in the way he voiced those two words.

Now that her initial surprise was over Salome instinctively stiffened. Her visitor was not one of her most favourite people. Not even remotely.

Michael Angellini was reportedly one of Sydney's most eligible bachelors, the wealthy owner of an exclusive Italian restaurant in King's Cross that Ralph had taken Salome to many times during the years of their marriage. In his early thirties, and handsome as the devil, he was no doubt all smooth charm to most of his women customers, yet right from their initial meeting, or soon after she'd been introduced as Mrs Diamond, the restaurateur began treating her with a cold, almost exaggerated formality that had made her seethe inside. She had learnt to feel nothing but contempt for those people who classified her on sight in that predatory female category including women who married older men for money.

Yet, oddly enough, Salome found a perverse pleasure in their frequent visits to Angellini's, taking pride in not showing her antagonism to this narrow-minded, prejudiced man. Quite de-liberately, she would give him a sweet smile and then be extra-attentive and flirtatious with Ralph, revelling in the feeling that she was throwing the Italian's unwarranted derision right back in his face.

He, however, found it very hard to hide *his* feelings, her presence always putting a tight, sour look on his face. Though this didn't mar his undeniable male beauty. The man's Latin ancestry had produced the sort of dark, brooding looks that women drooled over: strong, sculptured features; piercing black eyes; lustrously wavy black hair; a cruelly sensual mouth; and an elegant, arrogant grace that turned a dinner-suit into a lethal weapon.

Not that Salome drooled. The underlying antagonism she felt for him made her totally immune to his powerful sex appeal. There could have been a time when his brand of overt virility might have turned her head—she'd been as silly as the next young girl at sixteen and seventeen. But by the time she'd met Ralph, a few weeks short of her nineteenth birthday, she'd been cured of the irrationality of her adolescent hormones once and for all. Ralph's dignified maturity and lack of sexual aggression had been like a breath of fresh air to her.

True, she'd been initially worried by his age, but he had been a very determined man and had courted her with an old-fashioned respect and decency that she'd found both captivating and highly flattering. Heavens, here was this multi-millionaire, handsome, intelligent, powerful, who could have any woman he wanted. And he had wanted *her*!

Of course she hadn't known his secret back then... Still, even if she had known all along, Salome believed she still would have fallen in love with him. He had made her feel so very, very special, right from the start. Michael Angellini, however, never made her feel special, she thought, swinging angry eyes up to him. He never evoked anything in her except a simmering fury.

As was the case right now.

'Yes, it's me.' Her tone was curt, her words clipped. 'What is it you want?' she demanded. 'How did you get up here anyway? Oh, no! Don't tell me *you* live in the other penthouse?' The building was so large that the top floor had been divided into two huge luxury penthouses.

He sucked in an indignant breath, expanding his considerable chest beneath the pale blue sweater he was wearing. 'I'm afraid so,' he admitted with cold civility. 'I was out on my balcony just now, and thought I heard someone scream out. Naturally, I was concerned. Of course, I didn't realise *you* were in here, Mrs Diamond. I thought this was your ex-husband's apartment.'

The implication was quite clear. Anyone else, and he would come to the rescue. But *she* could scream her head off and he wouldn't turn a hair.

'This happens to be *my* apartment now,' she told him tartly, before she realised what the man had actually said. Cursing herself for her stupidity, she slipped off the chain and pulled open the door. 'You've *seen* Ralph recently, have you?' she demanded, uncaring now if they liked each other or not. If this man had some information about Ralph, then she wanted it. Here at last she might find some answers.

Her visitor looked startled, his black eyes flashing astonishment as they flicked over her face. 'You've been *crying*!' he said, almost accusingly.

Now it was Salome who was taken aback. For she had already forgotten her recent tears. 'Yes...no...I...' Damn it all, what was the matter with her? Did she have to go all helpless and confused, just because he was shocked to find that a calculating bitch like herself could cry?

'Does it matter?' she flung at him. He blinked. 'All I want to know is when was the last time you saw Ralph?' she went on, her tone urgent.

He gave her a long, assessing look before speaking. 'A few weeks ago.'

'Do you mean at the restaurant or here?' she persisted.

'*You* were with Ralph the last time he came to the restaurant, and that was well over a year ago.'

'Oh...' She frowned and chewed her bottom lip. 'It was here, then?'

'Yes. We run into each other occasionally. But what's this all about, Mrs Diamond? Surely you've been in touch with your ex-husband personally if this penthouse is now yours?'

'No,' she admitted. 'I haven't...I...' The lump gathering in her throat appalled her. The last person in the world she wanted to break down in front of was *this* man. 'I haven't seen Ralph for fourteen months,' she finished in a strangled voice.

Sympathy did strange things to Michael Angellini's face. It made him almost human. His mouth softened. And his eyes, which were usually as hard as flint, melted to a liquid ebony, washing over her with a look of surprising warmth and pity.

And then he did something else that stunned Salome. He touched her.

Oh, it wasn't an intimate, or a bold caress. He merely reached out his hand to curve lightly over one shoulder. But it seemed to burn a hand-print on the skin beneath her dress. She froze, her eyes widening, her lips parting slightly.

'I think, Mrs Diamond,' he was saying, his hand tightening before releasing her tingling flesh, 'that you could do with a drink. You seem very stressed. Why don't you come along to my place, where I can get you something to settle your nerves?'

Salome stared at this man whom she had always detested, unable to get her mind off her response to his touch. Surely it couldn't have been a *sexual* response? *Surely* not!

'Are you all right, Mrs Diamond? You look . . . odd.'

'Yes, yes, of course,' she snapped in confusion.

A single dark eyebrow lifted and those black eyes hardened again. 'Of course,' he drawled. 'Well, would you like to have a drink with me? Or would you rather be by yourself?'

Salome gave the darkly handsome face a hurried once-over, and was comforted to see she now felt nothing. Nothing at all! She sighed with relief. It had been shock, that was all, shock that her long-time foe had extended an unexpectedly sympathetic hand. No doubt she was susceptible to sympathy at the moment.

But the thought insinuated that he might have misinterpreted her reaction to his touch, and might even now be sizing her up as easy meat for his bachelor bed. The incident with Charles that morning had shown her that a man didn't have to *like* her to lust after her.

'You don't have to feel obliged to accept,' he said curtly as he noted her swift frown. 'I won't be offended in the slightest. I merely thought you looked like you could do with some company for a while. Believe me, I *do* realise you have never found my company to your liking in the past.'

Salome bristled. 'What came first,' she bit out, 'the chicken or the egg?'

He stared at her for a moment, then laughed, drawing her gaze to his dazzling white teeth and the attractive dimple in his chin. But there was no laughter in his eyes. They remained as hard and cold as ever. For some reason this annoyed her even more than usual.

'I think, perhaps, that I will take a rain-check on the drink,' she said with an icy hauteur that belied her agitated pulse-rate.

The laughter died on his lips, his strong jaw clenching tightly. 'Don't be so ridiculous,' he grated out. 'All I'm suggesting is that we have a drink together. Not another damned thing!' Looking away, he ran an angry hand through his hair. 'I'm not a masochist,' he muttered under his breath, before swinging his eyes back and adding more loudly, 'I thought you were anxious to hear about your ex-husband. Look, let's have no more silly arguments. Where are your keys? Aah...I see them.'

With that, he strode inside, picked up the keys from the coffee-table in the centre of the living-room, and returned, ushering her firmly outside and locking the door. Then, taking her elbow, he guided her along the hall, shepherded her through an open door, and deposited her on a cream leather sofa that was identical to the one in Ralph's unit.

'There!' He left her and strode over behind the glass and chrome bar that curved around one wall. 'That wasn't so hard, was it?'

Salome opened her mouth then snapped it shut. She couldn't trust herself to speak just yet.

A 'masochist'? she was fuming, her excellent hearing having picked up his low comment. Low, in more ways than one. If that wasn't the insult to end all insults. Brother, was she fed up with the way men perceived her. Fed up to the eye teeth!

Unfortunately, this particular man had information she wanted, so it wasn't in her interests to give him a blast of her Irish temper at that moment. But, by God, if he came out with another of those clangers, she was going to let him have it! And it wouldn't be the softly spoken, elegant Mrs Diamond he would have to contend with, but Salome Twynan, street-wise and tough, a fighter from her earliest years, a girl who'd had to be, just to survive!

CHAPTER TWO

'So!' Michael deposited two crystal tumblers on to the glass top of the bar. 'What will you have to drink? Your usual?'

Salome stared at him.

'My dear lady,' came the dry remark, 'you don't have to look so surprised. You and your husband were regulars at my restaurant for years. It's my job to familiarise myself with my clientele's likes and dislikes. I wouldn't be much of a host if I hadn't absorbed the fact that you only drink vodka and orange before dinner, and dry Riesling or white burgundy with your meals.'

He pushed the long sleeves of the blue sweater up his arms, showing surprisingly little body hair, and glanced at the gold watch on his wrist. 'Since it is now approaching five, I merely guessed the vodka and orange.' Those cold black eyes lifted. 'Was I wrong?' he drawled. 'Or have your tastes changed in the last year?'

Salome's green eyes flashed as they locked on to his hard gaze, certain that there was an underlying innuendo in those last words. Clearly he thought that, as Mrs Diamond, she had cleverly catered her tastes to what Ralph had liked, since he too had been fond of vodka and dry white wines. No doubt Mr Jump-To-Conclusions Angellini was now anticipating that such a professional gold-digger as herself might have moved on to the next man already, and adapted her likes and dislikes accordingly.

A type of black humour curved her lips back into a seductive smile. 'Why don't you just pour me something *you* like?' she purred. 'I'm sure you have *excellent* taste.' She gave him a heavy-lidded glance, thinking viciously that if he was fooled by such blatantly feigned behaviour then he deserved to be!

He glared at her for a moment, then gave a dry, hard laugh. 'Come now, Mrs Diamond,' he scoffed. 'You don't really expect me to fall for the batting eyelashes and husky-voice trick, do you? Save it for an older, more vulnerable prey—one who'll be so dazzled by your beauty that he won't notice the dollar-signs clicking over behind those gorgeous green eyes of yours.'

He folded his arms and frowned at her. 'You puzzle me, though. You're a clever woman—an expert, I would have imagined, on the male psyche. I can't believe you seriously thought that I would be so gullible. After all, *I* know that *you* know I've never been blind to your—er—chosen vocation in life.'

Salome could have reacted several ways. With a burst of true temper. Dignified outrage. Frozen silence. Even tears. She chose none of them. A cool smile crossed her lips and she had the pleasure of seeing a shocked look pass over her adversary's face. 'To be honest, it was an on-the-spot performance,' she confessed bluntly. 'A test, so to speak. But I'm relieved to see you came through it with flying colours. God knows how I would have coped if you hadn't.'

His back stiffened, his arms slowly unfolding to grip the edge of the bar, a barely controlled fury smouldering in those normally cold black eyes. The fact that she had finally got under his skin soothed Salome's own suppressed anger.

'But you were right about one thing, Michael, dear,' she went on. 'Your company is *not* to my liking, and neither am *I* a masochist. I came along here with you merely because I wanted to hear news about my husband.'

'*Ex*-husband,' he reminded her harshly.

'Whatever.' She uncrossed her legs and got to her feet, unable to sit there sedately any longer. She tried to keep a calm exterior, but inside her blood was well and truly up. 'If you're not going to have the decency to tell me what you know without any added insults,' she said curtly, 'then just say so and I'll leave.'

He didn't say so. He just stood behind the bar, staring at her. Salome got the oddest impression that with her firm stance she had achieved more in changing this man's opinion of her than she'd been able to do in her years as Ralph's wife. There was a look of grudging respect in his eyes as they moved slowly over her.

'I see there's more to you than meets the eye, Mrs Diamond,' he said at last.

She snorted. 'Am I supposed to be flattered by that remark?'

His laugh was very dry. 'No. I guess not.'

'Then would you kindly put me out of my misery and tell me what you know about Ralph?'

Again she was on the end of a sharp look. 'And *are* you in misery about your...about Mr Diamond?'

She shook her head in exasperation. 'Wouldn't *you* be, if the person you were married to chucked you out one day without so much as a word of explanation, then refused to see you?'

'I would,' he admitted slowly, 'if I really loved that person, and knew I hadn't done anything to instigate such behaviour.'

Salome gritted her teeth. 'Oh, of course,' she ground out, 'that couldn't apply to me, could it? I'm Delilah and Jezebel all wrapped up in one, aren't I? The sort of vampirish female that ensnares older men into her sexual clutches in order to fleece them of every cent, then tosses them to the wolves when the game grows tedious or a better meal-ticket comes along?'

He was clearly startled by her verbal attack, but recovered well to shrug nonchalantly. 'You said that. I didn't.'

'But you've been thinking it all right,' she flung at him. 'You thought it the very first night Ralph took me to your rotten damned restaurant!'

He glared at her, eyes hard again. 'You have to admit you did a good impression of the vacuous sex-object wife, married to a man old enough to be your father!'

'Age has nothing to do with love,' she argued. 'And I wasn't vacuous. I was shy. Tongue-tied...'

'Oh, come now,' he scorned. 'Shy? Tongue-tied?'

'Yes,' she insisted. 'At first.'

'Well, you soon learned what was expected of you,' he pointed out caustically. 'I've never seen such an accomplished courtesan, dripping all over your escort, eating him up with your eyes, laughing deliciously at every joke he made. And the *clothes* you wore. Or *didn't* wear, more accurately. Hardly the way a *shy* woman would dress!'

A fierce blush coloured Salome's cheeks at the essence of truth behind this accusation. Ralph had always chosen her clothes, and he had a penchant for evening wear that was very sexy. Low necklines and bare shoulders meant that underwear had always been at a minimum. Neither could she dismiss the fact that on subsequent visits to Angellini's she had often gone over the top with her flirtatious behaviour towards Ralph out of some sort of spite of their host's ever-reproachful eyes.

'I was always perfectly decently dressed,' she defended staunchly through her inner fluster. 'And decently behaved. Ralph was my husband, and you had no right to sneer at me behind his back.'

'I never sneered.'

'You could have fooled me!'

'Apparently I did!' he snapped.

They both glared at each other, the silence electric. And then he did the strangest thing. He sighed, his face softening, his eyes almost apologetic.

'Look, let's stop this,' he said reasonably. 'It's rather childish, don't you think? If it makes you feel better, I apologise. Now calm down and sit down. I'll get you that drink.' He gave a wry laugh. 'I think you might be more in need of it now than before.'

For a moment Salome stood where she was, feeling somewhat stunned. But then she slumped back down on the sofa, for she had begun to shake with spent emotion. What on earth was wrong with her, letting this man goad her into defending herself so hotly? What did it matter what he thought of her? He meant nothing to her, nothing at all! The only issue at stake here was trying to find out what she could about Ralph, yet she had allowed herself to be totally side-tracked.

Irritated, she glared over at Michael's now superbly composed self, silently going about mixing the drinks with efficient, economical movements. Cubes of ice were dropped in first, followed by a hefty slurp of vodka. Finally the glasses were topped up with fresh orange juice from the small bar fridge. She watched him walk round the front of the bar, grudgingly admitting that he looked almost as good in casual clothes as he did when dressed formally.

The softly moulding crew-necked pullover showed that his broad shoulders were not an illusion of good tailoring, the wool's blue colour highlighting his dark colouring. Salome's gaze drifted downwards to where his trim hips and long legs were housed in a pair of loosely fitting grey trousers. It annoyed her when she began to wonder what he would look like in a pair of tight, body-hugging jeans.

'Here we are,' he said, scooping up the brimming drinks without spilling a drop, and bringing them over with the skill and ease of an experienced waiter.

Which is probably what he once was, she thought caustically, before reminding herself that they had a lot in common, in that case. She had been a waitress before marrying Ralph. It bothered her momentarily that her years as the wealthy and privileged Mrs Diamond might have turned her into some sort of snob, since Salome Twynan would never have looked down her nose at someone for doing *any* kind of a job at all.

Don't be silly, she berated herself. You have every reason to feel bitchy towards this man. It has nothing to do with what job he's done, or hasn't done!

'So you really have no idea why Mr Diamond ended your marriage?' Michael asked, giving her a penetrating look as he handed over her drink.

The intensity those black eyes could project unnerved her. 'None,' she admitted.

He sat down on the sofa next to her, his own drink moving to his lips, those same disturbing eyes watching her closely over the rim of the glass.

Salome tried desperately to ignore how his gaze and closeness were affecting her. She felt stifled, nervous, afraid even. Of what? she puzzled frantically. Because she was alone with him in his apartment? Michael Angellini didn't seem the type of man to make a crass pass unless given *some* encouragement. He was, on the surface at least, a gentleman.

Salome pushed aside her illogical apprehension and put her mind back on the issue at hand. 'I came home one day,' she explained somewhat reluctantly, 'and found my bags packed. Ralph gave me no explanation other than to state that our marriage was over.'

The man next to her was clearly taken aback. He straightened and just stared at her, his glass hovering at his lips. Salome sipped her own drink, her hand shaking slightly.

'I...I tried to find out the reason, but he wouldn't budge,' she went on agitatedly. 'In the end I suppose I got a little hysterical. Ralph simply called one of his body-guards and had me removed from the premises.'

'My God, that's appalling!'

The depth of disgust Salome saw in his face startled her. Yet it was oddly comforting to have someone else find Ralph's behaviour inexcusable. Even her own mother had presumed she had been to blame. But then, poor Molly always thought women were to blame when a relationship ended.

'As I said to you earlier,' she managed to get out, 'I haven't seen Ralph in the fourteen months since that day. Not that I haven't tried.' And she found herself relaying to her surprisingly intent listener all her endeavours to have a personal meeting with her ex-husband.

'So, you see,' she finished, 'I'm anxious to hear anything about Ralph at all. I want some answers. I *need* some answers!'

'Of course you do,' he agreed strongly. 'Of course. No one deserves to be treated like that!'

Not even a gold-digging little tramp like me, Salome added silently with a weary sigh. Strangely enough, all of a sudden, this man's low opinion of her hurt. It hurt like mad. Ralph might have been able to snub his nose at the opinion of others, but Salome was finding it increasingly upsetting to have people believe she was little better than a woman of easy virtue.

An involuntary shudder ran through her, bringing a puzzled frown from her companion. 'Is there something wrong with your drink?' he asked.

It was just as well, Salome realised bitterly, that she had grown expert at the art of the superbly bland social face, which consisted of totally unreadable eyes and a soulless smile.

Yet, somehow, hiding the hurt this man kept dishing out, however unconsciously, proved to be more difficult than usual. That plastic smile just wouldn't come, and when she looked at him she found herself becoming lost in those incredible black eyes of his, which at that moment were filled with a disarming sympathy. She dragged her own away, and stared down at the half-empty drink.

'No,' she said tautly, twisting the glass around and around in her hands. 'It's fine.' She gulped most of it back in one go, then cleared her throat and looked up. 'You're being very nice to me, Michael. Considering...'

For a second he just looked at her, but she thought she detected a hint of irony in his eyes. He reached to pick up his own drink once more, turning his eyes back to hold her nervous ones with consummate ease. 'My friends call me Mike,' he said quietly.

For a second Salome was taken aback. Then she laughed. 'I'm not a friend, though, am I?'

He smiled and shrugged. 'You could become one.'

'I doubt that very much.'

'Why?'

Her expression was incredulous. '*Why?* For one thing, you don't *like* me!'

'Aah...' His smile became quite cynical. 'I can't deny that I didn't like you much when you were Mrs Diamond. But as...Salome's your name, isn't it?'

'Y-yes,' she admitted warily.

'As single Salome, I think I could like you well enough,' he stated with a seductive softness, then leaned back and took another swallow of his drink.

Salome's insides tightened. Was this what she'd subconsciously been waiting for, been agitated about? For her one-time foe to make a sexual move towards her? Her glare was withering. 'I suppose I'm going to have to get used to that sort of remark,' she snapped. 'But I would have thought that a man as eligible as yourself wouldn't have to resort to chasing frustrated divorcees.'

There was a sardonic lift to one eyebrow. 'And *are* you frustrated, Salome?'

'Oh, for goodness' sake!' She stood up and slammed her glass down on to the low marble-topped table in front of the sofa. 'I'm not going to stay here and exchange sexual innuendoes.

Obviously your offer of friendship was nothing but a ruse. You couldn't give a damn about helping me with news of Ralph. All you really want is to get me into bed!'

He stared at her for what seemed like ages, then a wry smile tugged at his lips. 'Let me assure you, my dear Salome,' he drawled, 'that such a thought has never entered my head. Of course,' he added, his gaze travelling slowly over her heaving breasts, 'I wouldn't knock you back if you offered. Or aren't you *that* frustrated?'

'Oh!' she gasped. 'Oh!' she repeated with a stamp of her foot. 'Of all the——' Flustered and fuming, she whirled on her heels and began striding towards the door.

'Mr Diamond always had the same young woman with him.'

Salome froze mid-stride, then turned. So there *was* another woman, a new 'project' for Ralph to work on, a new 'possession'. Funny, she would have thought she'd be relieved to find an answer at last. Instead, she still felt devastated. Yet there she'd been lately, thinking her love for Ralph had finally begun to die.

'A—a young woman?' she repeated blankly.

'Yes. A brunette. Attractive. Very well-groomed. A career girl, by the look of her. Though I have to confess I don't think they were business acquaintances. Fact is,' Michael went on quite ruthlessly, 'there's no doubt in my mind they were lovers. I saw them come out of the penthouse very early in the morning together a couple of times. Once they had their arms around each other in the corridor.'

Lovers?

Salome stared, a weak hand fluttering up to her throat as she tried to make sense of Michael's observation. How could Ralph have a lover? Unless ... unless he had lied to her ...

Salome felt quite ill, the blood draining from her face, her eyes dropping to the floor. Why would he have done such a thing? *Why?*

'Come and sit down.'

Salome's head jerked up when gentle hands closed over her shoulders. How had he got to her side so quickly? The last time she had looked he had been sitting down.

'Come on.' He led her over and settled her on the sofa. 'I'm sorry, Salome. I shouldn't have told you that quite so bluntly. I didn't re-alise——'

Her head snapped up, green eyes pained. 'Re-alise what?' she said brokenly. 'That I might really care about my husband? That I might actually be upset to find he was probably being unfaithful to me all along?'

He crouched down on his haunches in front of her, his hands gripping hers. 'Maybe Mr Diamond has a lover now. But I *don't* believe he would have been unfaithful to you while you were still living together.'

The fierceness in his voice and eyes startled her. 'I can't imagine any man having a woman like you in his bed,' he continued, 'and looking elsewhere.'

For a second she almost laughed at the complete irony of his remark. Till she realised exactly what his words implied—that, as a supposed 'professional' at the art of lovemaking, she should be well equipped to hold a man's interest.

It infuriated her that she kept on feeling distressed by this man's bad opinion of her. No way, however, was she going to show that he had upset her again.

She still laughed, but it reeked of sarcasm. She also snatched away her hands. 'What a typically superficial male comment! No woman is *that* good. Somehow, I expected more of you, Michael Angellini, than to believe sex alone will hold a man indefinitely. Or is that all it takes to hold *you*?' she couldn't resist adding.

Those black eyes glittered dangerously as he got slowly to his feet, glaring down at her. She had hit a nerve all right with her comment. And serve him right! she thought savagely. She'd had a few nerves hit by him over the years. She lifted her chin defiantly to glare back up at him. Think of me what you like, her eyes taunted. I don't give a damn!

'Actually, you're wrong, Salome,' he bit out. 'Sex, alone, does not hold me. I wish it did,' he grated out, throwing her a black look as he dropped down in his corner of the sofa. 'At least sex is straightforward and simple. It's when it gets tangled up with deeper emotions that the trouble starts.'

Salome found herself feeling an odd sympathy for him. He sounded genuinely wretched, as though he had suffered deeply from an unhappy love-affair, and was still suffering. She didn't like to see anyone on the end of that kind of distress—even Mike. She knew how it felt.

She darted a quick sidewards glance at his grimly set mouth, and wondered if that was why he hadn't married. Perhaps he loved some woman who didn't love him back? A measure of guilt crept in as she realised she might have done him an injustice. Not that she felt he deserved an apology. He'd always given more than he got. Besides, they had once again got off the point of why she had come along here.

'So,' she said bitterly, 'Ralph isn't suffering from a hideously disfiguring disease after all.'

Her host shot her a startled glance.

Salome shrugged. 'It was another of my way-out theories for why Ralph threw me out.'

'I see,' Mike nodded. 'Well, I'm afraid to say Mr Diamond looks as fit as ever, though I can't say I like his new hair colour. I prefer a man to go grey gracefully.'

'He's dyed his hair?' The idea astounded Salome. Admittedly Ralph had always been vain about his thick brown hair, but the grey at his temples had never seemed to bother him unduly. No doubt he wanted to look younger to impress this new lover, she thought bitterly, then wondered with added misery how many others there had been.

'Yes, he's gone blond.'

'Good God!' She stood up, still shaking her head in confused desolation. 'Well...there's really nothing more to be said, is there?'

Her companion jumped to his feet. 'Don't go yet,' he said, his tone surprisingly urgent. Salome blinked her amazement up at him. 'Have dinner with me tonight.'

She gaped at him, unable to hide her complete and utter shock. 'You have to be joking?'

He kept a perfectly straight face. 'Not at all.'

'But—but why?' she stammered.

'Why not?' he persisted.

She gave a dry laugh. 'I think you know damn well why not.'

His eyes didn't flicker. 'You're going out with another man?'

She dragged a deep breath and counted to ten. 'No,' she said with barely held patience. This was too ridiculous for words.

'Ralph won't be dining alone tonight,' he inserted quietly. 'Why should you?'

She gave him a sharp look. 'That's playing dirty.'

A slow smile creased his mouth. 'There are times,' he drawled cryptically, 'when one has to resort to whatever weapons are at hand.'

Salome didn't have a clue what he was talking about.

'Come on, Salome. Say yes. It won't kill you. We'll call a truce for one night.'

'Oh, so you *do* accept that we haven't exactly been friends?' she pointed out drily. 'Nor are we likely to be while you hold the opinion of me that you do.'

'You could always try to convince me differently,' he suggested with a rueful smile.

'Huh!' She flicked a stray curl back over her shoulder. 'I'd have more luck convincing the Greenpeace movement to take up whaling.'

He laughed, and this time genuinely amused lights glittered in his eyes. Salome suddenly realised that their bantering was not malicious any longer. She was, in fact, quite enjoying the flow of dry wit between them. It surprised her.

'Come on, Salome. Stop frowning and say yes. I've only asked you out to dinner, not to marry me!'

There was a caustic flavour in this last statement that caused Salome to flare. 'Thank goodness for small mercies!'

He glared at her for a few seconds, his whole body tensing noticeably. But then he visibly relaxed, a ghost of a smile playing at the corners of his mouth. 'Tut-tut, you *do* have a temper, don't you?' He reached out and put a firm grasp on her elbow, and began leading her inexorably towards the door. 'Next thing you know you'll be changing your mind about going out to dinner with me.'

She ground to a halt, exasperation written all over her face. 'Might I remind you I *haven't* said yes yet?'

'Haven't you? I could have sworn you had.'

Though obviously put on, his air of bewildered confusion had a certain charm, and Salome found herself smiling. 'Do you ever take no for an answer?'

A slow smile came to his mouth. 'Not often.'

'Perhaps I should refresh your memory on what it's like to be turned down,' she challenged.

His smile turned faintly sardonic. 'It wouldn't be the first time.'

'I'm surprised. I would have said a man such as you would have an impeccable track-record with the ladies.'

He shrugged. 'You can't win them all, I suppose.'

Salome thought she caught an edge of pain in those words, and she remembered her previous impression that Mike could well be suffering from a broken heart. Unexpectedly, it touched her. She didn't like to think of anyone having to suffer what she'd been suffering.

This line of thought also made her realise he might be thinking the same about her, and that this invitation to dinner could very well be a true gesture of kindness. Yet here she was, being difficult and stroppy about it. She resolved to give in graciously and be done with it.

'Very well,' she said with a resigned smile. 'I'll come. Just this once.'

He seemed pleased. 'Great. What time will I come along and pick you up?'

It suddenly dawned on her that he thought she'd moved into the penthouse, so she launched into the explanation that she didn't intend living in the penthouse but would probably sell it, and that she lived with her mother in a neat, three-bedroom brick cottage in the suburb of Killara.

Now he didn't seem so pleased, a dark frown drawing his black brows together. Salome deduced somewhat caustically that his Christian charity in asking her out clearly didn't extend to a twenty-minute drive both ways through busy, city-bound traffic.

'If it's too much trouble...' she began.

'No, no—no trouble.' But the frown had not entirely disappeared. 'Just give me the address and a time to be there. By the way, do you have any preference where we eat?'

'Not Angellini's,' she said instinctively.

'Certainly not.' His tone was even sharper than hers, and she actually winced. It was peculiar enough going out with a man who had once despised her, and maybe still did! She certainly didn't want to return to the scene of the crime, so to speak.

A thought struck her, though, that hadn't occurred to her before. 'Don't you have to act as host at your restaurant tonight?' she asked. He'd always been there, if her memory served her correctly.

'Not on a Thursday.'

'Oh...' Her eyes dropped, her heart regretful all of a sudden that she had agreed to go out with him. He was a link with her past, with Ralph, a past she now wanted to forget. Her ex-husband must be some sort of monster, to deceive her as he had done. She actually cringed as she thought of how she had allowed him to dictate every facet of her life. God, she'd been the original puppet on a string, the perfect piece of clay to mould as he willed. And all the while he'd been making a fool of her, having lovers behind her back while she fulfilled the role he'd chosen for her—that of a decorative hostess with no more say in their life than one of the original paintings he hung on his wall.

Salome shook her head as she vowed never to surrender herself to a man's will like that again. If she ever remarried it would be to a man who would be her partner, not her master—an equal in every way.

Her eyes lifted to see a ruthless black gaze peering down at her, the gaze of a man whom she suspected would be no more husband material for a woman than Ralph, obviously, had been. For a moment she felt oddly disconcerted, but quickly dismissed the unwarranted reaction. This swinging bachelor's personal life was no concern of hers. 'Well, Mike?' she said. 'Have you got a pencil and paper, or an excellent memory?'

CHAPTER THREE

SALOME'S mother came into her bedroom as the former was putting the final touches on her make-up, and gave the large suitcase sitting beside the door a disgruntled look. 'Just because I asked Wayne to move in,' she flung at her daughter in a petulant tone, 'doesn't mean you have to move out. I thought you were happy enough living here with me.'

Salome counted to ten, afraid that she wouldn't be able to keep the angry frustration out of her voice if she answered straight away. When she'd come home and found her mother had asked her latest boyfriend to share not only her bed but the whole house, Salome had seen red. It wasn't that Wayne was a bad sort. He was probably the best type of man Molly had ever been out with.

But Salome couldn't bear to stay around and witness her mother make the same old mistakes with yet another man. So she had drastically revised her plans, telling her mother some white lies about the unit and car, saying she had decided to keep them both and live in the unit.

Actually, this was not entirely untruthful. Given her new situation, Salome could see that to leave herself destitute was insane. It was all very well to be high-principled, but she could see, finally, that she had gone too far in giving away *all* of Ralph's settlement. Her marriage to him, after all, had cost her four years' wages. So she'd decided to take the equivalent sum from the money the sale of the unit brought, and buy herself a modest unit somewhere. The same applied to the Ferrari. When she'd met Ralph she had owned an old run-about, which he'd disposed of, so she believed she was justified in using some of the money from its sale to purchase a modest vehicle.

All these plans, however, she kept to herself. It was far easier to let her mother think she was keeping the lot. Less argument. Less hassle.

Molly had been astonished though delighted with what she called her daughter's finally coming to her senses about keeping something from that 'old coot!' Not so delighted, however, about her moving out, for they had become very close over the last year, all their old differences seemingly having been resolved.

Till now.

'Please, Molly,' she said calmly. 'Let's not argue about it. I'm not exactly moving interstate. I'm only a twenty-minute drive down the highway, and I'll visit often.'

'Oh, I get the picture. Wayne's just an excuse. It's this Mike Angellini you're going to dinner with, the one whose unit is next to the one Ralph gave you. You've set your sights on him, haven't you?'

That was so ridiculous that Salome almost laughed.

'Not at all,' was her rueful reply as she picked up the bronze lip-gloss. 'I told you. Mike's an old acquaintance. I've known him for years. You don't honestly think that after what I've been through with Ralph I'd leap into another involvement this quickly, do you?'

'Who knows what you'd do?' her mother said archly. 'Any girl who could marry a man thirty years older than herself could do anything!'

Salome counted to ten again. 'Not all women like younger men,' she said with creditable control.

'Younger men are more fun,' Molly stated pompously. Then grinned.

Salome shook her head in fond exasperation and began putting more pins in her up-swept hairstyle. Her mother's behaviour with men frustrated the life out of her, but it was impossible to dislike the woman. Or not feel sympathy for the events that had shaped her life. An abandoned child, and the product of various state institutions, Molly was a teenage runaway, pregnant by the time she was fifteen, Salome's father an Irish sailor who'd been in Sydney for a week on shore leave and had never returned.

Molly had always claimed to have loved him. But then, Molly claimed to love *all* her boyfriends, even creepy Graham, who'd been twenty-three to her thirty-three, and spent more time chasing the eighteen-year-old daughter than the mother.

Salome glanced in the mirror at Molly, who was still very attractive at thirty-eight and not as rough in speech and manner as she used to be, and wished with all her heart that this time she'd found the right man, the one who would marry her.

'How old *is* this old friend of yours?' Molly asked, dropping down on the end of the single bed. 'Not as old as Ralph, I hope?'

'Early thirties.' Salome stood back from the dressing-table mirror, and made a final survey of her appearance. The forest-green woollen suit, with its softly pleated skirt and fitted single-breasted jacket, suited her tall, shapely figure to perfection. And the ivory silk blouse with the tie at her neck looked suitably demure.

There would be no cleavage tonight, Salome had decided. No way did she want to spend the evening having Mike Angellini either glaring reproachfully at her breasts, or assuming from her mode of dress that he *might* be on to a good thing.

That was one of the reasons, too, why she had put her hair up, being aware that some men found long, loose hair sexually provocative. Maybe she was being overly careful, but she had a feeling that the evening could be spoiled if she gave Mike the wrong impression. As she'd found out to her chagrin that morning in Charles's office, a man's desire had little to do with admiration of a woman's real personality. All a female had to have was a pretty face and a nice figure to interest a male on that level.

'Is he handsome?' Molly kept on.

'Very.'

'Not married, is he?' Her mother's voice carried suspicion.

'No,' Salome laughed. 'For pity's sake, quit the third degree, will you? You'll make me nervous soon. Look, I can't even get my earrings in now!'

Actually, underneath her composed façade, Salome *was* beginning to feel a bit nervous. Odd, really. Over the years as Ralph's wife she had dined with princes and sheikhs, gone to the races with royalty, sailed with tycoons, and partied with movie stars. Why, then, should she be worried about a simple dinner for two?

Perhaps it wasn't the dinner itself she was nervous about, but what Mike would think when he arrived and she told him she had decided to move into the penthouse after all. In fact, was moving in *tonight*! She could hardly explain the real reason without embarrassment. Nor could she, in front of Molly, reveal that it was only a temporary arrangement, till the unit was sold.

Hopefully he wouldn't take her abrupt change of mind as meaning she was interested in him, as Molly had suggested. She had a suspicion that he wouldn't need much encouragement to try to change their platonic date into a less platonic one.

Another disturbing thought popped into her mind. Perhaps he didn't need any encouragement. Perhaps a man as handsome and eligible as Mike *expected* his dates to end the evening in bed with him. She hadn't thought of that.

Salome had no idea what men expected on a date these days. She'd had to put up with a lot of groping as a teenager, and even then boys had expected a girl to come across pretty quickly. She'd had many a wrestle in the back of a car during her dating years, but only once had she

given in—the summer she'd turned seventeen.
And of course she had thought she was in love.
The man in question had been older than her
usual dates. At twenty-four, he'd not been prepared to take no for an answer.

But sex had not been the earth-shaking experience Salome had been expecting. Physically
she'd felt nothing after the initial stab of pain.
It had been a non-event. Things hadn't improved
either, on subsequent occasions, and her boyfriend had quickly dumped her, saying she was
abnormal. Salome had been very upset at the
time, the only consolation to her lack of pleasure
in sex being that she didn't have to fear she might
turn out to be as promiscuous as her mother.

Nevertheless, when Ralph had come along and
proposed his platonic marriage, Salome had initially been perturbed. Underneath, she hadn't
given up hope of finding the right man one day,
with whom she would be a normal woman,
finding satisfaction and enjoyment in making
love. But Ralph had been persistent with his
flattering attentions and declarations of love and
caring, and in the end she just hadn't been able
to say no. After all, he'd covered her main ob-
jection by promising that if she ever wanted a
child she could have one by artificial insemi-
nation or adoption.

And, as it turned out, Salome had never really
felt that the lack of sex in her marriage had been
any great sacrifice. Admittedly, she did have
bouts when she was restless and couldn't sleep,
but she didn't believe that had anything to do
with physical frustration. She'd always been a bad

sleeper. She wouldn't even have associated her insomnia with such a cause if Ralph hadn't suggested it once.

She would never forget the occasion. It had been the first night Ralph had taken her to Angellini's. She had come home still flushed and fuming with fury at Michael's high-handed attitude. Ralph had floored her by saying that her anger was sexual, that the Italian's high-voltage sex appeal had stirred her blood, that she was angry simply because she wanted him. She recalled laughing at the time. The idea was ludicrous!

Perhaps not so ludicrous now, though, she thought, her mind slipping back to that moment earlier in the day when Mike had touched her...

With suddenly trembling fingers, she had difficulty securing the gold and pearl studs in her ears, her mind still elsewhere as she automatically applied perfume to the pulse-points at her wrists and throat—a musky oriental perfume that she always wore.

'You look lovely, dear,' her mother complimented.

Salome snapped out of her disturbing reverie to realise she had been staring in the mirror without focusing. She did so now, studying her reflection and wondering what it was about her that men found so attractive. She didn't think she was that beautiful. Her face was triangular, her chin slightly squared off at the point, her nose straight with flared nostrils that suggested an unpredictable temper. Nothing irresistible there, she thought ruefully. Her hand came up to trace her high forehead and cheekbones, then dropped to run dismissively over her far too generous mouth.

She couldn't see why men so liked her hair either, that wild mass of burnished curls which resisted taming no matter what any hairdresser did. Even now, piled securely on top of her head, dozens of tiny curls and tendrils were already escaping.

She scowled and saw that annoyance darkened her almond-shaped green eyes to the colour of slate. Set deep and wide, they were perhaps her best feature, though, without mascara, the long pale lashes were inclined to be insipid. She almost cringed to think how she'd used to make them up, with thick black eye-liner and buckets of mascara. At the moment, however, enhanced by smoky green eye-shadow, grey eyeliner and mascara, her eyes looked exotic and mysterious.

'The eyes of a temptress', Ralph used to say, then smile at her.

Those eyes clouded over and she no longer saw her reflection. A wretchedness was clutching at her heart, a bitter taste coming to her mouth. What kind of cruel game had Ralph been playing with her?

'Mr Angellini doesn't stand a chance.'

'What?' She turned around, her face blank, her mind still distracted.

A coughing sound in the open doorway had both women looking around. Wayne was standing there, dressed casually in a navy tracksuit, a lazy grin on his large pleasant face. Salome had only met him a couple of times before, but, while she thought her mother was making the same old mistake in letting the man move in with her, she had to admit he was Molly's best bet yet. Around forty, and in the building trade, he had an air of solid decency about him that her mother's other boyfriends had lacked.

'There's a chap at the door looking for you, Salome,' he drawled. 'And a Jag at the kerb. Better shake a leg or he might do a flit. He doesn't look like the sort of bloke who'd have to hang around waiting for birds too often. Don't you be long either, Doll,' he directed at Molly, and, without a second glance at Salome, ambled off back down the hall towards the living-room.

His physically ignoring Salome made him go up in her estimation a thousand-fold. You never knew, she thought ruefully. Maybe Molly had cracked it at last.

She smiled at her mother, who was lifting her eyebrows up and down in mock fun. 'A Jaguar, no less,' she teased. 'Glad to see my daughter hasn't dropped her standards.'

'Now, Molly, I've already told you, I——'

'Yes, yes, I know; he's just a friend. I won't keep on about it. But you will look after yourself, won't you, in that empty old penthouse?'

Her gentle tone choked Salome up. 'Of course,' she managed to get out.

'And forget silly old Ralph,' came the firm advice.

'I'll try, Molly. I'll try.'

Mike had apparently been content to wait for her on the front doorstep, but when he saw her coming down the hall, carrying the heavy suitcase, he stepped inside into the light of the foyer to help.

Molly literally caught her breath and ground to a halt, staring at Mike as though he were Tom Cruise in the flesh. Salome could understand her mother's reaction, even if she didn't approve. Her own heart had jolted when she'd seen him.

There was no doubt that black did something for Mike Angellini that no other colour did. Not that he was in his dinner-suit. The black woollen suit he was wearing was far less formal—in fact so incredibly modern that Salome was rather taken aback. She had always imagined him to be a very conventional dresser.

But apparently she was wrong. For there was nothing conventional in the loose, front-pleated trousers and the equally loose, cardigan-style jacket. Certainly nothing conventional in his decision to matching both of these with a chest-hugging white polo-necked sweater, either. He looked rakish and dangerous and devastatingly sexy.

Salome's green eyes remained outwardly calm as they flicked over the tall, smiling figure moving towards her, but her heart was missing the odd beat, and forming in her mind was the awful suspicion that any immunity she'd once had to this man's attractiveness might be on the wane.

'You've decided to move into the penthouse?' he asked her as he took the suitcase out of her hands.

Salome looked up into eyes that betrayed definite satisfaction at this thought, and an ominous apprehension joined her suspicion. 'Yes,

yes, I—I am,' she stammered most uncharacteristically.

'Great.'

He glanced over her shoulder and gave Molly the full benefit of a dazzling smile. 'If you tell me this lovely lady is your mother,' he drawled, 'then I won't believe it. She's much too young.'

Salome found herself flashing him a caustic look before she could stop herself, but Molly blushed prettily. 'I had Salome when I was very young,' she said sweetly.

'You *must* have.'

Salome stiffened, a tightness coming to her chest. She was hating this exchange, hating it so much that she was shocked at herself. Surely she couldn't be jealous—could she?

'People often mistake Salome for my sister, not my daughter,' Molly was saying coyly.

'I can imagine,' was the suave reply.

Angry green eyes snapped to Mike, but he was busy smiling at her mother. Her glare landed on his stunningly handsome face, his sensual mouth, his dancing black eyes, and quite suddenly her fingers itched to slap him.

A gasp of shock brought both her mother and Mike staring at her.

'Something wrong, dear?' Molly asked, blue eyes concerned.

'No, no, I—er—I just realised I forgot my credit cards. I can't live without them.' And she fled back down the hall, racing into the privacy of her room.

The reflection of herself standing just inside the door, clutching her handbag to her chest as if it were a life-line, stared back at her from the dressing-table mirror. She looked most peculiar, she thought, her normally pale complexion flushed, her green eyes brilliant and wide, her lips slightly parted.

Salome walked numbly over, and stared into the mirror. Whatever had happened to her out there? Slowly, she put the handbag down on the dressing-table, a deep frown coming to her brow. Was it jealousy? Anger? Or simply a burst of exasperation over the possibility that, if Mike kept up the false flattery, her mother would be imagining herself in love with *him* next?

Yes, she decided with a flood of relief. That sounded spot on. Molly's predilection for younger men had been a trial all Salome's life. Not that she seriously believed Mike would be interested in her mother. Men like him went for the younger, more glamorous type.

Which reminded her... It would be wise to be on her guard with Mike tonight. All of a sudden he was exuding the sort of charm Italian men were renowned for, and which she'd seen him use on women other than herself. Now that their hostility towards each other had been put on hold, it was on the cards that he might fancy a spot of seduction for supper.

A bitter smile passed over her lips. Silly man. There were better bets than her in that regard. Much better. Still...it didn't do any harm to watch herself. Mike was an exceptionally attractive and sexy man, and it was hard not to respond, even if that response was fleeting and superficial.

It suddenly occurred to her that she had left him out there with Molly alone, and she scuttled out of her bedroom, walking quickly back down the hall, her handbag under her arm.

'Found!' she announced with a hurried smile. 'Just as well, or the entire bill would have been on you tonight, Mike.'

Those black eyes locked on to hers, amusement in their depths. 'My dear Salome,' he drawled lazily. 'When I take a woman out to dinner I *always* pay.'

Salome had to drag her eyes away from the magnetism of his, her heart thudding against her ribs. 'I'll come back and get more of my things tomorrow, Molly,' she said far too breathlessly. Really, this sudden susceptibility of hers to Mike's male charisma was beginning to annoy her. 'Perhaps we should be going?' she suggested, lifting cool eyes. Thank the lord, she thought with sardonic relief, that I've learnt not to show my emotions in my face.

Nevertheless, Mike slanted her a thoughtful look before smiling at her mother. 'Nice meeting you, Molly. You and Wayne will have to come out with Salome and myself one night. What do you say, Salome? Will you be in on that?'

Salome smothered a sigh, wondering just how much Molly had told Mike while she'd been in the bedroom. No doubt he already knew about her illegitimacy and her mother's new live-in boyfriend—Molly was not high on tact. Although, to give him credit, Mike wasn't looking down his nose at Molly, as Charles had done.

Even Ralph, she thought wryly, had wanted her mother kept safely in the background.

But Mike's easygoing acceptance of Molly and Wayne did not excuse his presumptuous invitation a moment ago. Truly, men could be the limit! Would it damage his ego to admit this was a one-off platonic date? And did he *have* to put on that lady-killer act, just for the benefit of her mother?

Piqued and irritated, she literally had to plaster her smile in place. Already, it was feeling like cement, and she suspected that, any moment, cracks would begin to show. She had to get out of here, and right now!

'That would be nice,' she agreed with forced sweetness, then turned to her mother. 'See you tomorrow, Molly,' she said as she bent to plant a kiss on her cheek.

'You too, love. And you know what they say...' Molly threw after them as they made their way out on to the porch and down the front steps. 'If you can't be good, be careful!'

Salome groaned under her breath. Molly had always had this embarrassing fondness for that type of sexually flavoured comment.

'Should we stop at a chemist's on the way?' Mike chuckled. 'Or shall we be daring and leave matters up to fate?'

An angry exasperation welled up inside Salome, but she bit her tongue till they were beside the white Ferrari in the shadows of the tree-lined driveway, then she turned to set steely eyes upon her escort.

'Let's get one thing straight, Mike,' she said curtly. 'I'm going to dinner with you tonight because you were quite kind to me today, and because I thought this was your way of apologising for your narrow-minded dislike of me all these years. But I don't want you to get the idea this is going to become a habit, just because I'm moving into the penthouse next to yours. Also, let me assure you that when I go out with a man on a platonic date I *don't* need to buy contraceptives!' She glared at him in what she imagined was dignified reproach.

His head tipped slightly to one side, his expression one of mild pity. 'Poor Salome...I can see that your recent divorce has destroyed your sense of humour.'

'Really?' Her tone was very prickly.

'Yes, really.' He put down her case next to the Ferrari, and slipped his hands into the pockets of his trousers. 'I wasn't suggesting a thing. I was having a joke, merely following on from your mother's quip, that was all.'

There was a weary note to his voice that made her feel guilty. Looking at the situation more objectively she realised she had over-reacted abominably. 'I see...I—I'm sorry, then,' she said, then added defensively, 'But I was worried that you might be having after-dinner expectations.'

' "Expectations"? What kind of "expectations"?'

'*Sexual* expectations!' Good grief! Why did she have to blush when she said that? Thank the lord the light was dim here.

'Ahh...'

A dark, predatory light gleamed momentarily in his eyes, bringing immediate panic. 'I won't sleep with you, Mike Angellini!' Salome burst out, and was relieved that her words sounded firm. Not as rattled and shaky as she was feeling.

His laugh was low and drily amused. 'I don't recall asking you to. Anyway, I told you once before, Salome, sleeping with you is not high on my list of priorities. Look, we'll have to get a move on,' he said, deftly changing the subject. 'Our booking was for eight-fifteen, and the restaurant I'm taking you to is back at McMahon's Point. Have you got a key for this boot, and I'll put your case in?'

Salome stared speechlessly up at him for a moment, her mind in total confusion. She should have been pleased to be on the end of such a blunt rejection, but she wasn't. She felt annoyed.

'Your key?' Mike repeated, his voice betraying a growing impatience. 'You have to follow me in your car, remember?'

Salome snapped out of her startled bemusement with a degree of fluster. She had difficulty finding her key, and when she handed it over she was astonished to see her hands were trembling. Mike gave both her hands, then her face, a sharp look, but took the key and deposited her case in the boot.

'Keep close,' he advised as he handed back the keys. 'I wouldn't want to lose you in the traffic.'

'Yes...yes, I will,' she assured him, her voice not at all steady.

Again his eyes raked hers. 'Truce still intact?' he asked with a wary little smile.

'I suppose so,' she choked out.

'Mm.' His frown showed he didn't quite believe her, but then he shrugged and strode off towards where his bronze Jaguar was parked at the kerb. Almost against her will, Salome's eyes followed him, lingering on the breadth of his shoulders, the feral grace of his stride, the way his glossy black waves gleamed lustrously under a streetlight. Her stomach fluttered as a thought struck. Was it possible that Ralph's accusation had finally come true—that she did indeed now want this man to want her? Was that why she'd been jealous when he'd paid attention to her mother, then angry when he'd told her he wasn't interested in her in that way?

No, she decided, frowning and shaking her head. No...that wasn't possible. That didn't make sense. I won't accept that, she argued with herself. Basically, we dislike each other. It's just female vanity, that's all. No woman likes a man to say outright that he doesn't want her. Yes, that sounded right. I'll put it down to a case of female pique.

A shiver ran through Salome as a puff of wind blew down the driveway, rustling the leaves at her feet.

'You like standing out there in the cold, do you?' Mike called to her over the bonnet of his car.

Salome looked up and pulled a face at him. 'Hardly.'

'Look...' His voice was gaining a frustrated edge. 'I realise you don't really want to go out with me, but you can't very well trundle back

inside now, can you? And you have to eat somewhere, so come on, get that sexy bod of yours
into your white charger and move it! And remember, if you're too slow I'll lose you.'

Throwing her a challenging look, he ducked
into the car.

Her green eyes blazed angrily Mike's way, but
he was already behind the wheel, the Jaguar
growling into life. Taking up the challenge,
Salome followed suit, jumping into the Ferrari
and firing the engine with a furious flick of her
wrist. When the Jaguar shot away from the kerb
with a squeal of tyres, she was hot on its tail.

CHAPTER FOUR

THERE were several sticky moments on the way to the restaurant when a lesser driver could easily have lost the Jaguar in front. But Salome didn't. She stuck to its gleaming bumper-bar like glue, letting neither amber traffic lights nor changes of lane faze her. In an odd sort of way, it was the most exhilarating experience she had had in months, even if more inspired by temper than a natural love of speed and danger.

She was normally a very safe and careful driver. Tonight, though, she seemed driven by inner demons, and, by the time she screeched the Ferrari to a halt beside Mike's Jaguar in the restaurant's car park, her own engine was as hot and bothered as the car's.

What on earth was possessing her tonight? she thought dazedly as she slumped over the wheel, her heart pounding madly.

Any agonising over this score had to be postponed, however, for at that moment her door was wrenched open, making her sit bolt upright. Mike leaned across her and angrily switched off the still throbbing motor, his black eyes blazing. 'Good God, woman, do you always drive like that?' he snarled.

Salome bristled to her own defence. 'You said not to lose you,' she pointed out, 'and you didn't exactly dawdle yourself.'

The exasperated man gripping the car door with white-knuckled intensity wasn't to be denied. 'Maybe so, but I didn't mean for you to drive the whole damned way barely five centimetres from my back bumper-bar. Hell, you scared the living daylights out of me every time I changed lanes or went around a corner! I was too bloody petrified to slow down in case I finished up with you in my passenger seat!'

'You needn't have worried.' Her tone was now unruffled and very, very droll. 'Ralph sent me to an advanced driving school before he gave me this car, his motto being that all expensive and beautiful things should only be put into the hands of people who know what to do with them.'

Salome retrieved the keys from the ignition and slipped them into her handbag, then glanced up to find Mike still glaring down at her, his eyes more disapproving than ever. What had she said *now* to annoy him?

'Excuse me,' she sighed, swinging her knees around in order to climb out of the low-slung car. He took a step back, at the same time holding out his hand to help her. There seemed no option but to accept it.

His grip was firm, hauling her upwards in a single smooth motion which brought her within inches of his lean length, her hand squashed in his between them. She blinked up at those intense black eyes, and was suddenly very aware of the hard male body close to her own softer female curves. The subsequent fluttering in her pulse-rate startled her. As did the quiet heat that crept over her skin.

Heavens! She knew Mike was a very attractive man, but it was infinitely disturbing to find he could command such a response from her without even trying. What would happen if he *did* try?

Prior to this moment, Salome would have sworn that no man would have had a chance in Hades of seducing her unless she was in love with him. Now, amazingly, Mike was stirring her on a purely physical level as no man had ever done before. Really, it was incredible! But it seemed there was a first time for everything, she thought bitterly.

Well, she would just have to ignore it all! came her immediate resolve. Or who knew what might happen? As Mike had said to her earlier that afternoon, he might not have fancied her seriously in the past, but he wouldn't knock her back if she offered herself to him on a silver platter.

A shudder raced through Salome at the thought of ending the night in his bed. Casual sex was not for her. She had seen the results of a woman letting men use her in that way. All she had to do was to keep thinking of Molly, and this unexpected weakness was sure to cure itself.

Gathering her inner resources, she sucked in a resolute breath and plastered a determinedly innocuous smile on her face. 'Shall we go inside?' she suggested, and slipped her arm through Mike's elbow.

A shaft of relief darted through her when this bold foray produced no feelings whatsoever. No tingling nerve-endings, no increased heartbeat, no flush of heat to the skin. Marvellous! The cure was working.

'Am I missing something?'

She gave Mike's disgruntled face the most innocent look. 'Pardon?'

'You seem very pleased with something all of a sudden. Am I to be allowed in on it?'

'I'm sorry,' she blinked vapidly. 'I don't know what you mean.'

He withdrew his arm from hers and gave her a sharp look. 'Don't take me for a fool, Salome,' he warned darkly. 'I know when a woman has devious thoughts ticking over in her brain. And I know when she's trying to hide something.'

She gave a light laugh, but underneath she was genuinely worried. Mike was an astute and intelligent man. And a dedicated womaniser, if the gossip she had heard about him was correct. Had she unwittingly given something away a moment ago? She hoped not, but, if she had, the best thing was to try to confuse the enemy immediately.

'Surely you aren't imagining I'm planning to replace Ralph with you, are you, Mike?' she teased, green eyes mocking.

His black gaze narrowed. 'Hardly.'

'Then stop glowering at me. You're quite safe. All I was thinking earlier was how strange it was that *you* should be the first man I'd go out with after my divorce.'

Too late, she realised that even this was an admission.

His left eyebrow lifted. 'I find it hard to believe I'm your first male escort since Ralph.'

She silently thanked his distrust of her. 'Well...' She let her voice trail away tellingly, but her heart was in her mouth. 'One doesn't always go *out*...' She considered it the lesser of two evils if he thought she'd had a lover or two. Better than his jumping to the conclusion that he alone had captured her sexual interest in fourteen months.

Mike's mouth tightened at this revelation, his gaze hardening to the cynical expression she had known and hated from her nights at Angellini's. It was depressing that any ground she had made in changing his opinion of her had probably been lost, but it couldn't be helped. Perhaps it was just as well, anyway, since he was to be a neighbour, that he be kept at a distance. Doubtless, after tonight, he wouldn't be rushing to ask her out again.

'I suppose I should have known better,' he drawled, 'than to think a woman like you would do without—er—shall we say male "companionship", for want of a better word?'

Salome buried any hurt beneath a wall of bitter sarcasm. 'My, my, you do have a high opinion of me, don't you? One wonders what you're doing here with me at all. Or were you thinking of sacrificing yourself later tonight to appease my—er—"loneliness", for want of a better word?'

A muscle in his jaw clenched, then released to make way for a black smile. 'My neighbourly offers of friendship don't usually extend quite that far.'

'Oh, dear, I'm crushed.'

'Of course, I wouldn't like to see a lady suffer. If the worst came to the worst, I suppose I could always lie back and think of Australia.'

'Don't you mean England?' she countered tartly.

'Poetic licence. Look, do you think we could cut this charming repartee short till I can get some food into my mouth? I haven't eaten for hours and I'm in dire need.'

'By all means,' she tossed back. 'I happen to be hungry too, otherwise *I* wouldn't be here.'

He chuckled. 'Come on, then. I know when I've gone as far as I can go. Dinner it is!' And he took her arm.

Salome was quite happy to be stampeded across the car park in blissful silence. She had felt her blood-pressure rising dramatically beneath her increasingly tart replies. Though not from temper. The cause was far more perturbing.

Mike's retort about lying back had projected a vivid and erotic mental image into her imagination, sending the blood roaring through her veins. Even now her mind's eye held a tantalising vision of him, naked and supine on her bed. He wasn't alone either. *She* was there, making the most amazingly abandoned love to him.

Shock rippled deep inside Salome. It was incredible! Impossible! This couldn't be *her* thinking things like that! It wasn't as though making love had ever brought her any physical pleasure. Why should she be craving it with *this* man all of a sudden?

Yet, as her eyes slid sidewards to flick surreptitiously over him, she was consumed by urges so wanton and so primitive that she had to bite her lips to stop herself from groaning out loud. Currents seemed to be racing down her limbs into her fingertips and toes. A clamminess was spreading over her skin. Her mouth felt dry, her lips needing moisture.

As for her breasts...Salome was bitterly regretting her decision not to wear a bra. As it was, she was fiercely conscious of the movement of her breasts as she walked, the way her nipples were rubbing to painful hardness against her clothing.

'I know this place doesn't look much,' Mike remarked as they approached the windowless façade of the restaurant, 'but it improves once inside.'

Salome dragged her mind out of its dungeon of horrors to really look at the building for the first time. It was a solid square two-storeyed structure, painted an unprepossessing dark brown, with 'MARTINE'S' in gilt letters over a heavy-looking wooden door.

Mike moved ahead slightly up the front steps, the door yielding reluctantly to his push. He held it open and waved her inside. Salome stepped into the dimly lit, air-conditioned interior, her whole insides twisted as tight as a coiled spring. The door closed behind her, giving her an entombed feeling. She glanced around nervously as Mike drew to her side.

He was right about the restaurant. The interior was quiet and dark and intimate, with a small black and white tiled lobby, a classy-looking bar on their left, a flight of stairs straight ahead, and offices, Salome guessed, behind the closed door to her right. An attractive dark-haired woman in her late thirties and a smart black dress floated down the stairs, smiling at Mike as she approached. 'Mr Angellini,' she murmured with a gracious nod. 'Your usual table has been reserved for you.'

Salome's agitation was momentarily distracted when she followed the woman to the top of the stairs and realised why Mike had chosen this particular place to eat. Clearly, it wasn't far from their block of units, since the wide windows on the upper floor displayed the same splendid view Salome had seen from her penthouse balcony that afternoon. Except that now it was night-time, with Darling Harbour, the city and the bridge ablaze with lights, their glittering reflections dancing in the black waters that lapped the foreshores.

Salome hesitated only briefly to admire the view before continuing her trek between the tables at the woman's heels. Her eyes automatically noted and assessed the quality cream tablecloths and napkins, the comfortable cane-backed chairs, the silver candlesticks and the assorted potted palms placed discreetly for extra privacy. A place of class, without being ostentatious.

They were shown to the most private table of all, tucked away in a dimly lit corner, but still with an unimpeded view, a reserved-for-Angellini card propped up against the silver candlestick. Recalling the woman's words that this was Mike's *usual* table sent an ironic little smile to Salome's lips. This was not his usual sort of date, though, was it?

Salome no longer had the slightest worry about Mike making a pass at her tonight. She knew he wouldn't. Beneath his drily amused tolerance and neighbourly goodwill, he still despised her morals. It was all rather a sick joke, the way she kept wanting him, despite everything. He would probably laugh, if he knew.

Once they were seated, their hostess handed out the menus, lit the single candle, then asked if they would like a pre-dinner drink. Mike glanced questioningly over at Salome, but all she could think of was how brilliantly his eyes gleamed by candle-light and how sensuous his mouth looked in shadow. 'Salome?' he prompted.

Oh, God! she thought despairingly. 'My usual,' she managed huskily, guilt and shame a heavy burden in her heart. How could she be thinking and feeling these things for a man who thought so lowly of her? On top of that, she was supposed to be still in love with Ralph! It was all very confusing.

Mike ordered her a vodka and orange, and a double Scotch on the rocks for himself. The woman departed saying she would bring the wine list and take their orders when she returned with the drinks.

Once alone, an awkward silence fell over their table, with Salome deliberately averting her eyes from his too intuitive ones to stare blankly at the panoramic view.

'How far are we away from home?' she asked after a while. But she still didn't look at him.

'Only a couple of blocks.'

'And you come here often?'

'Often enough.'

Composed now, she swung her eyes back to face him, and was surprised to find she was able to look at him in a perfectly calm manner. See him for what he is, Salome, she told herself. A womaniser. A worse user, even, than Ralph. Maybe that will exorcise you of these unwanted and unwarranted desires.

'You've had a lot of women, haven't you?' she said casually.

He seemed startled by her question, leaning back in his chair and studying her for a few seconds before answering. She found the delay almost as unnerving as his close scrutiny. 'How many is a lot? Five? Ten? A hundred? And from what point are you counting? From my first fumbling encounter, or from the time I would classify myself as a passable lover?'

Salome began wishing she had not started on this subject. The thought of his making love to any woman was suddenly agitating her. Silly, really. What did it matter? It seemed, though, that this tack was certainly not curing her. Far from it.

She gave a nonchalant shrug. 'Please yourself.'

'Oh, I usually do,' he drawled. 'Which means I decline to answer your question on the grounds that it might incriminate me. Unless, of course, you want to play mutual confessions... How many men have *you* had, Salome? Or have you lost count?'

She stiffened, but then laughed. '*Touché*. But I claim the same privilege as you, Mike. You already think I'm Mata Hari. I wouldn't want to shock you further.' And shocked he would be, she thought ruefully, if she said she'd only had one man, and that man was *not* her husband! Not that he'd believe her.

The drinks arrived at this fortuitous point, and Salome resolved to keep their conversation off sex for the rest of the dinner. It wasn't easy, but she managed, chattering away about the weather and sport during the entrée, politics during the main course, music and theatre over dessert, then the state of the economy all through coffee and liqueurs. Salome could not have told anyone afterwards what she actually ate. Seafood, she supposed, since it was primarily a seafood restaurant.

Occasionally, she caught her companion giving her a frowning glance as though he didn't know quite what to make of his remarkably well-informed companion. Salome smiled to herself at the irony of *his* confusion. Her own was far more unnerving.

It was past eleven by the time Mike announced they should be going. She stood up much too abruptly, and swayed on her feet.

'Are you all right?' he asked solicitously.

'The wine has gone to my head a bit,' she said, clutching the back of her chair.

'Here... take my arm. What you need is some fresh air.'

'Fresh air' was putting it mildly. It was bracing and cold, a stiff breeze coming off the water. But at least it was sobering. Not that Salome had drunk all that much. She hadn't. A couple of glasses at most. Perhaps it was the company that was so intoxicating, she thought tartly as Mike led her across the car park, his thigh brushing against hers with each stride.

'Are you sure you're capable of driving?' he asked.

'Perfectly,' she stated with conviction, knowing she wasn't over the legal limit and desperately wanting some respite from his physical nearness.

Still, she drove very carefully back to the apartment block, trailing after Mike's Jaguar from a safe distance, and parking in slow motion in one of her allotted spaces in the basement car park. Mike carried her large case over to the single private elevator that operated from that level, using his key to operate the locked doors. Salome sighed as the doors whooshed shut and the lift began its rapid climb to the penthouse floor. A few minutes and she would be able to crawl into bed, taking her fuzzy head and wretched feelings with her.

Halfway between the fourteenth and the fifteenth floors, the unthinkable happened. The elevator shuddered to an unscheduled halt and the lights went out, plunging everything into darkness.

CHAPTER FIVE

IT TOOK a few seconds for Salome to grasp what had actually happened. She stood frozen and disbelieving, hoping against hope that the lights would snap back on and the elevator would resume its smooth ride upwards.

But darkness reigned supreme. Darkness, plus an unbearable silence.

'Blast!' Mike muttered after what seemed like ages. 'You OK, Salome?'

'Y-yes.' No, I'm not! she wanted to scream at him. I'm terrified. I don't want to be locked away here in this small space in the dark with you for what might be hours. Oh, God, I was almost there... in my own place... safe and sound...

'You don't sound as though you're all right,' he said, his tone concerned. 'You're not claustrophobic, are you?'

Only when I'm with you! 'I don't know,' she choked out. 'I don't think so, but this has never happened to me before.'

'Mmm... I guess there's been some sort of electrical failure. Do you remember which side of the doors that emergency telephone was on?'

Was he mad? Good lord, she didn't remember a damned thing about getting into this steel coffin with him except how long and elegant his fingers were when he pressed the buttons! 'Er—no,' she admitted huskily.

72

'I think it was the left.'

A vivid expletive broke the stifled atmosphere as Mike tripped over the suitcase. Salome huddled into a far corner so that he wouldn't trip over her. *That*, she could do without!

'Here it is,' he growled. Some more rummaging sounds and a metallic click. 'There's a dial tone. Hello? Hello? Anyone there?'

Another silence, punctuated by Mike's heavy breathing. Or was it her own?

'Anyone there, dammit?' he continued irritably.

More silence.

He kept trying for some time, but no saviour answered. Finally, he put the receiver back with a weary sigh. 'I'll try again later. Don't worry, Salome, someone must know what's happened. We'll get out of here eventually.'

She didn't realise he couldn't see her shaking her head.

'Salome?' A hand brushed over her nose.

'Yes, I'm here,' she said hurriedly, and moved sideways out of the corner and away from his searching hand. He wasn't touching her now, but he was standing right in front of her. She could hear his breathing, smell his musky aftershave.

'Don't be frightened,' he soothed.

'I'm not.'

'You sound it.'

She sucked in a deep breath, then exhaled. 'I'm all right. Really.'

'Do you want to sit down? We could use your suitcase as a type of seat.' Common sense told her this was a practical suggestion, but she hesitated to give him permission to be pressed up against her. 'Come on,' he insisted.

She heard the sounds of his dragging the case up against the wall near by. Two firm male hands found her arms, pulled her over, and sat her down. 'Move along a bit,' he suggested as he tried unsuccessfully to fit beside her.

It was not the most comfortable of seats, with one of the side-locks sticking into her left buttock and the handle jammed against her hip.

'I think we should lie the case down flat,' Mike said after a minute.

They did so, and this was indeed more comfortable to sit on, but somehow more intimate, with their bodies being closer to the floor and their legs stretched out in front of them. Salome was clutching her handbag in her lap as though it would protect her against hidden invaders.

'Well,' Mike sighed after another awkward silence. 'What shall we talk about?'

'Do we have to talk at all?' she snapped.

She could *feel* the way his head shot round to stare at her through the blackness. 'I think you must be frightened,' he remarked drily, 'or you wouldn't be so snappy.'

'Don't be ridiculous! I'm not exactly pleased, but I'm not frightened.'

'If you say so.'

He said nothing after that, and in the end Salome could not take the sound of his quiet, even breathing any longer. 'You're not going to sleep, are you?' she said accusingly.

'Hardly.' She didn't miss the caustic tone in his voice.

Another couple of minutes ticked away in slow motion.

'Tell me, Salome, what *is* that perfume you always wear?'

She was about to answer when the word 'always' registered, and brought an unexpected quiver of alarm. Any man who recognised a woman's perfume as always being the same must have been taking rather special notice of her.

Not necessarily, logic dismissed. Mike was a connoisseur of women, and would notice such feminine trivia as instinctively as some men noticed makes of cars.

'It must have a name,' he persisted.

'Orient Mist,' she admitted curtly.

'Mm. Evocative... but then, it's an evocative perfume.'

Salome's breath caught at the low, almost seductive tone in his voice. Against her will, an erotic shiver ran up and down her spine, reminding her of how vulnerable she would be to this man if he decided to take advantage of the situation they were in.

'You're cold,' he observed when another shiver rippled through her. 'Would you like my jacket around your shoulders?'

'No, no,' she hastily protested. 'I'm fine. If I want anything extra I can always get something out of my suitcase.'

'Ahh, yes... our seating... Still, it is getting cool in here, and we'd be warmer like this.' He put an arm around her shoulder and drew her against him.

Horrified, she allowed it, for to pull away or cry out would have been more telling. But, oh...the feel of his body hard against hers was unbelievable! Tension gripped all her muscles, turning her into a mangled mess of misery and desire.

'Relax,' he murmured. She couldn't relax. She just couldn't. 'What's wrong, Salome?' he whispered, pulling away as he would to stare down at her. Except that in the darkness she couldn't see anything, her only physical sensation the feel of his warm breath close to her face.

'Nothing...nothing...I——'

There was no stopping her gasp when his hands found and cupped her face. 'You say nothing, but your voice is shaking and so is your body. If it's not our hapless situation or the cold, then what is it? Surely you're not afraid of me, are you?' His words had a slow, steady delivery in the dark, like relentless drips of water.

'No,' she choked out.

'Then why do you tremble so?'

This time she could find no words of protest, no denial for what he was about to conclude.

His ragged intake of breath still surprised her. 'So!' he exhaled, his fingers tightening their grip on her face. 'You're not as indifferent to me as you pretend. Or are you so frustrated tonight that you'd respond no matter who was touching you? Does the dark help? Can you block me out of your mind, pretend I'm one of those gigolo types you use whenever your frustration reaches unbearable proportions?'

'Don't,' she groaned when his thumbtips started stroking her lips.

'You don't mean that,' he rasped. 'You want this, want it quite desperately, if I'm any judge. And, by God, I'm going to enjoy giving it to you!'

Thinking back, Salome realised that if she had given him a cold rebuff instead of her pathetic little 'don't' he wouldn't have gone ahead, and she wouldn't have found out the disgusting truth about herself.

But she didn't do that, and from the moment his mouth met hers she was lost, lost to sensations she had never experienced before, lost to needs that had only ever been lightly touched on, driven by a force so strong and intoxicating that she was powerless to resist it.

Not that Salome took an active role to begin with. She didn't. She merely gave him access to her mouth, a robotic permission, as it were, to take her lips, to stroke them with his tongue, to press and probe at them till somehow they were open, as though shocked into it. And into that startled silent cavity he finally slid his tongue.

There was no harsh thrusting or demanding, just a persuasive, seductive exploration that set every nerve-ending tingling, that made her lips fall open even wider, till the corners of her mouth ached.

But it was an exciting ache that Salome would have endured willingly forever. She even moaned her disappointment when he finally withdrew, her fingernails digging into the leather of her handbag with a heightened tension that seemed to be gripping every extremity of her body. All she wanted was to have his mouth back on hers, to have his hands searching for and finding every hot, pulsating part of her body.

'You don't want me to stop, do you?' he said hoarsely.

'No,' she admitted, her voice shaking. 'No...'

His raw groan stunned her. Clearly, he wanted her almost as much as she wanted him. Maybe he had *always* wanted her. No, no, a dim memory refuted. That's not so. He *said* that wasn't so.

His next kiss obliterated any further thought, and this time his mouth contained nothing but uncontrollable passion, a taking rather than a tempting. Salome met him halfway, their tongues joining together in a violently sensuous mating that could only be eclipsed in one way. She had no doubt where they were heading, where these torturous kisses would end. No doubt. And much as a far distant corner of her conscience struggled to make her see the wrong and the danger, her body steadfastly refused to recognise any of it. It needed to do this, needed it with an intensity that was frightening because it was utterly and completely beyond her control.

They were slipping sideways on to the flat side of the case, Mike's weight pressing down upon her, when suddenly he made a grunting sound and wrenched himself away. 'What in hell's this?' he growled. The handbag was yanked roughly out of her hands and obviously flung aside with considerable force, for it thudded noisily against a wall.

Now his hands were back, pushing her right down across the case, her buttocks on one end, the back of her head falling off the other on to the floor. It was a crazily uncomfortable position for her, with one arm lying up the wall of the elevator, the other flung wide, yet Salome found it incredibly exciting. She liked the feel of his touch, possessive and masterful on her spread-eagled body, liked the way her impatient breasts were being thrust upwards into his impassioned hands.

She could hear his breathing, as heavy and ragged as her own, hear his dark mutterings as he began working on the buttons of her jacket and blouse, then the tie at her neck. Cool air suddenly caressed bare breasts, a rash of goose-bumps temporarily sobering her. For a split second the appalling truth of what she was allowing came home to Salome but, before she could react, Mike's mouth moved across her breasts and closed over one single, straining nipple.

A moan was torn from deep in her throat, the fingers of both her hands curling over to dig into her palms. 'Oh, God!' she whimpered. She jammed her fists down beside her on the case, but this only served to give her a lever with which to arch her back further upwards, pushing her flesh deeper and deeper into his mouth. Her head swam with dizzying pleasure, the blood in her veins surging hotly through her body.

Finally, when she thought she had felt every nuance of delight her breasts could possibly produce, he took one rock-like point between his teeth and gave it a not-too-gentle tug.

Salome's mouth fell open in a tortured gasp, the shaft of sensation slicing sharp and deep inside her. Her mind struggled to distinguish whether it was pain or pleasure.

Till he did it again.

Both! she realised with another gasp. Both...but she didn't care. All she knew was that she wanted it to go on and on. Madness! Insanity!

So Salome was startled when all of a sudden an incredibly warm and loving wave of emotion joined those other more electric sensations, impelling her hands to lift and splay into his hair, curling the silky strands round and round her fingers as she held him to her breasts as fiercely and possessively as a mother held an adored infant. Strange words of love hovered on her lips, dying to be spoken. She moaned in her battle to keep them at bay. Somehow, even in her dazed state of rapture, she knew the danger of telling this man she loved him. It wasn't true, anyway. Deeply embedded maternal instincts were confusing her. She didn't love him. She couldn't...

Perhaps he took her moans as a protest, for suddenly he stopped those tormenting little nips, and began licking her instead. She sighed, half relieved, half disappointed, though the feel of a moist and gentle tongue on those highly sensitised buds was oddly soothing. But, when a hand covered her knee and began sliding upwards, any sense of soothing disappeared, every nerve-ending instantly on alert.

Salome always wore suspenders, and she gasped when Mike's fingertips moved from the top of her stockings to feather across the soft flesh of her inner thigh. But he didn't linger there for long, his fingers homing in on the heat that was already searing its way through her panties. Her breathing ceased as he stroked the damp silk, tension and suspense at what he would do next holding her frozen.

There was no hesitation. His fingers slipped underneath, where he began to explore her with devastating intimacy. Salome could no longer hold her breath; the air punched from her body in gasps as she sucked in again and again for oxygen. Her heart was going at fifty to the dozen, blood pounding in her brain. She could feel her muscles clenching tightly inside, and while what he was doing was incredibly exciting, she began to get a glimpse of what it might feel like if he was really inside her, filling her, loving her.

'Mike,' she groaned.

She had forgotten his mouth was busy at her breast till he abandoned it and the air stung the moist bud.

'Yes, I know,' he muttered thickly. 'I know. I will...'

Suddenly, lights blazed overhead, the floor of the elevator shuddering beneath them as it lurched into an upward movement.

Glazed green eyes looked up into smouldering black ones, horror dawning instantly. Salome's head jerked up from the floor, her stricken gaze staring down at her semi-naked body, her dishevelled clothes, her knees, raised and evocatively apart. Mike was still leaning over her, his face full of recent passion and immediate frustration.

She threw at him what could only have been interpreted as a reproachful and damning glance. Immediately, that impassioned black gaze hardened, his cynical expression challenging her to deny that she had been a willing participant in all that had happened, and almost happened.

Salome knew she couldn't, which only increased her shame and self-disgust. But mixed with the feelings of humiliation was a righteous and indignant anger, for, in her opinion, he had indeed taken advantage of her and the situation. Hadn't she practically begged him not to kiss her?

Yet thinking about that first kiss now, and how quickly she had surrendered to his will, sent a humiliating heat to her cheeks. How could she have allowed such liberties, in a lift, of all places? As she uttered a tortured groan, Salome's right hand shot out to give him a hard push in the chest, and he fell backwards. 'Get away from me, you . . . you . . .'

'Cad?' he suggested drily as he levered himself from the floor.

A sob of fury broke from her lips. 'That word's too good for you!' she cried, her hands scrambling to do her jacket up over the gaping blouse, her only thought now being that at any second the lift would stop and those doors might open on to shocked eyes. Feeling sick to her stomach, she catapulted herself upwards, stumbling when her right heel buckled under her.

Mike steadied her with a hand on her arm, but she wrenched away, sending him another vicious glare. 'Don't you touch me!'

His eyebrows shot ceilingwards in mock surprise. 'Really! A minute ago you were begging me to. It just shows you the fickleness of some women.'

'You know damned well I would never normally let you even touch me, let alone...let alone...' A shudder of remembered disgust reverberated through her already shaking body. 'You took advantage of me! You...you knew I was in a vulnerable state about Ralph and that woman. You probably deliberately got me tipsy, all the time planning to...to——'

The lift reached the penthouse floor and the doors whooshed open.

No one was there.

Sighing, Salome sagged back against the wall, relief flooding through her. She couldn't have borne for anyone to see what her shame kept telling her must be obvious, with her tangled hair, her bruised mouth, her over-bright eyes, her disorganised clothes.

Though any relief was short-lived.

'You were saying?' Mike drawled. He had moved to stand with his back against the open doors, his arms folded, his harsh gaze merciless in its derision. Looking at him now, Salome found it incredible to believe that a minute ago she had been wanting him. At this very second she hated him, hated him for being able to make her feel what he made her feel, without love or caring. It was cheap and horrible and tacky. And almost beyond comprehension!

She had known earlier in the evening she was madly attracted to him, had even fantasised about making love to him, but the reality had been much more shocking. The speed of her surrender; the intensity of her feelings—the madness of it all!

All Salome could think of to explain it was that she must have changed, sexually. She had read of women like that, who became more interested in the physical as they matured, who started looking for sex for sex's sake, whose taste in men became overtly pointed in one direction. Her mother was certainly evidence of that theory, she thought bitterly. Perhaps she had indeed inherited the same weakness. It had only taken a man like Mike to bring it out in her.

An awful thought surfaced. Perhaps she had projected this new self to him this afternoon. Perhaps that was why he had asked her out in the first place, because he sensed this new vulnerability and frustration. Her mind flew to those earlier moments today when she had been agitated and not known the reason. Now she had to accept that she had probably been wanting sex even then!

Salome shook her head, appalled. This was the last straw, being plagued by urges she couldn't control. Ralph's treachery had stripped her of most of her self-esteem and respect. Now it seemed she was going to finish the job all by herself!

No way, she thought with a desperate burst of defiance. No way!

Dragging in a deep breath, Salome picked up her handbag and tucked it under one arm. She righted her case and, without so much as a word or a glance, marched determinedly from the lift.

With a predatory swiftness Mike's hand shot out to grab her wrist, swinging her round, making her drop both bags as she almost fell. 'I'm not letting you off that easily,' he snarled, hauling her upright in front of him. 'Oh, I realise you weren't letting *me*, Michael Angellini, make love to you in there in the dark. I was just a male mouth, a male hand, a male body. And now that the lights are on you've changed your mind. But that's too bad, darling, because I haven't changed mine. You've damned well teased me for years, and you're not going to do it again tonight!'

She stared at him, green eyes widening with shock. And indignation. '"*Teased*" you?' she repeated, stunned. 'I've never teased you!'

He gave a snort of disgust. 'Oh, no? Then what would you call the way you acted every time you came into my restaurant? There you'd be, half dressed and all over your husband like a rash, yet all the time making sure I was noticing what you were doing, flicking those seductive green eyes at me, that luscious mouth of yours always curved back in a sweet but treacherously knowing smile. Did it give you a kick to go home leaving me actually aching with frustration? Well, *did it*?'

The hand on her wrist tightened to yank her hard against him, his head dipping till his mouth was terrifyingly close. 'You knew I wanted you from the first moment we met,' he grated out in a low, hard voice. 'You used that fact to play a cat-and-mouse game with me, probably to arouse *yourself* so that you could stomach going home to sleep with a man you didn't love. But you made a mistake, Salome. *You* might be a cat, but *I'm* certainly not a mouse—something you're soon going to learn!'

Salome swallowed, her eyes blinking, her mind being bombarded with the most incredible and appalling thoughts. God in heaven, *had* he really wanted her all along? Even worse, had she somehow recognised this, and unconsciously responded even back then? Had Ralph been right about her anger being a substitute for desire? Shakily she recalled how she'd used to look forward to going to Angellini's, despite the derision she was subject to there. Then afterwards, in the car, she would definitely be on edge. And, though she wasn't sure, she suspected those had been the nights she couldn't sleep, tossing and turning till dawn.

Salome groaned and shook her head. If this was so, then her marriage had been a total sham on *both* sides. Not only had Ralph not loved her, but she hadn't really loved him either!

Everything inside her screamed out that this couldn't be true. She had loved Ralph. She *had*! In desperation, her mind focused on the one thing she could throw back in her tormentor's face. 'You said you had never wanted me! You said——'

His laughter cut her off. 'I said that I had never wanted to take you to bed, to *sleep* with you! And I didn't. A bed, I never envisaged, and sleeping was hardly what I had in mind. Hell, it was all I could manage some nights not to drag you out into a back room and take you there up against the door!'

All colour fled from Salome's face. 'You don't mean that. You couldn't——'

'I do and I could,' he growled. 'You want proof?'

'Dear God, don't!' she moaned, her eyes pained and imploring.

'Oh, for pity's sake stop looking at me like that!' he flung at her. 'Hell, I won't force you, though, damn it all, you probably deserve it!' With that, he flung her away from him. 'Go on, get out of here. Go. You're not worth it!'

Stunned, shattered, Salome stood there for a moment, dazedly rubbing her throbbing wrist. Mike snatched up her case and her handbag, and shoved them into her hands. 'Here... now *run*, woman, while you're still in one piece!'

Turning blindly, she stumbled down the corridor to her door. Somehow, she located the keys, and eventually found herself inside, leaning with her back against the door. Then she slid down to the floor and started to cry.

Much later, her heart heavy, her senses dulled by physical and emotional exhaustion, she stripped herself off and stood robotically beneath a tepid shower. Too tired to unpack and find a nightie, she climbed naked between the sheets of the double bed in the main bedroom, lifting a weary hand up to snap off the bedside lamp, plunging the entire place into darkness.

But before her mind could embrace the mental darkness of sleep, it drifted inexorably back to that moment when Mike had threatened to prove his passion for her and she had groaned for him not to.

A further groan broke from her lips, and she turned to bury her face in the pillow. For now that she was alone, now that Mike was no longer a menacing presence, Salome could admit that the new, sexually aware part of herself had wanted him to prove it, however and wherever and as often as he wished, this realisation having shocked her sufficiently into making one last desperate plea. Fortunately, he had been decent enough to answer that plea.

So for now she was safe. For now . . . But what of tomorrow, and the next day, and the next?

Mike wanted her, and he was not a man who would give up easily. It might take weeks for this penthouse to be sold. And all the while Mike would be living next door.

The only solution, she finally accepted, was to move back home with her mother. A wave of depression swamped Salome. Why was all this happening to her? All she'd ever wanted in life was to be secure and reasonably happy, and to avoid the sort of emotionally tormented and draining existence she'd had to endure with Molly during all her growing-up years. Now, just as she was getting over the harrowing effect of her divorce, she'd been thrown back into a maelstrom of mental torment, not only besieged by the hurt of having to face the ugly truth of Ralph's betrayal, but also tortured by a physical desire she didn't want and couldn't understand.

The future loomed ahead of her as a maze of misery, with no hope for the peace of mind she had always craved.

Thank the lord tomorrow is my rostered day off, she thought with a sigh. Perhaps I won't go in to work to make up for today. I just want to pull these blankets over my head and never surface again.

But Salome *was* to surface from those blankets again, far sooner than she would ever have envisaged, and with a far greater threat to her happiness...

CHAPTER SIX

ONE second Salome was fast asleep, her mind in oblivion. The next, she was awake, her eyes dazzled by the overhead chandelier.

Her first muddled thought was that she must have left the light on. Pushing her tangle of curls back out of her eyes, she glanced at the time on the bedside clock-radio. One thirty-four. It was then that she saw Charles, standing in the bedroom doorway.

Salome sat bolt upright and simply stared at him. He looked drunk, his cheeks flushed, his greying hair untidy. He was also clearly contemptuous at finding her there.

Salome clutched the quilt up towards her throat, her green eyes wide with shock.

'I thought you said you didn't want this place,' he muttered derisively.

His beady, bloodshot eyes raked over her bare shoulders, then dropped to where alarm was making her breasts rise and fall rapidly beneath the bedclothes. A glittering came into his gaze that made Salome feel sick to her stomach. If she hadn't been so stunned by the situation she might have thought to get out of bed, to *do* something. But she stayed where she was, huddled under the sheet.

'Funny,' Charles slurred, 'I never imagined you sleeping in the raw. I always pictured you in tan-

talising black lace, or virginal white silk.'
Chuckling obscenely, he drew out a packet of cigarettes and lit one, then stuffed the packet and lighter back into his suit pocket. The smoke curling around his head made him look even more menacing, his piggy eyes dark and dangerous as he leered at her through the haze.

Salome swallowed and tried to gather her wits. She was not stupid, and it didn't take her long to gather that Charles held duplicate keys to this penthouse and had been using it as a sort of dosshouse. And much as logic demanded that a high-profile lawyer wouldn't risk his career and reputation by doing anything criminal—like raping her—no amount of common sense seemed to be able to stop fear and panic from clutching at her throat. So much so that she couldn't even find her voice.

Finally, Charles levered himself away from the door-jamb, stubbing the cigarette out on the wall before he strolled across the beige shag carpet towards the bed. Salome felt her insides cringe, even though she didn't move an inch. Don't show any fear, she kept telling herself. He's just trying to frighten you. He won't really do anything.

He reached the bottom of the bed and idly picked up a corner of the quilt. Her fingers tightened on her end, uncomfortably aware of her nakedness beneath the bedclothes. Why, oh, why, she groaned, hadn't she unpacked a nightie?

'If you're nice to me,' he drawled, 'I'll tell you why Ralph kicked you out.'

Salome's heart jumped, then tightened again. 'I already know,' she said brusquely. 'And I have no intention of being nice to you, Charles Smeaton. Not now, not *ever*! I don't like you sober and I especially don't like you drunk!'

Charles dropped the quilt and set cold eyes upon her. 'Is that so?' Those beady grey eyes raked over her once more. 'Well, that's just too bad.'

Panic was threading its way through Salome's system, but she kept a brave, bold face turned towards her intruder and slowly eased herself back to sit hard up against the headboard, dragging the quilt with her. 'If you don't leave immediately,' she advised curtly, 'I'm going to have to tell Ralph. I don't think he'll be too pleased with your having kept a set of keys to this place.'

The returning smile was so confident that Salome was rocked. 'Quite frankly,' Charles countered, 'I don't think Ralph would give a stuff at my using this place. And, since you know why he finished your marriage, you'll know he has other things on his mind right now.'

Salome shuddered, and that ghastly smile widened. She was scared, and he knew it. In fact, he seemed excited by it, his face flushing all the more. Uncontrollable lust peered out at her, smouldering and strong and sadistic.

Now Salome felt true panic. Aroused and intoxicated, Charles looked incapable of realising the serious consequences if he forced himself upon her. There was no point in screaming, she decided with a rapidly escalating pulse-rate. Without any windows or doors open, no one would hear. Not even Mike next door. These penthouses were solidly built for privacy.

Her eyes slid towards the en-suite bathroom across the room. If she could make it in there, she could lock the door.

Charles's laughter was low and ugly. 'I don't think so, Salome. I'm a lot closer than you.'

She pretended she didn't know what he was talking about. 'Closer to me than what?' she said scoffingly.

Again he laughed. 'OK, play that game if you want to. Play *any* game you want to. I like games. My favourite is hard to get. Nothing like a bit of challenge to whet the appetite.'

When he actually began loosening his tie, Salome's face paled. 'I want you to get out, Charles!' she demanded, but her voice was trembling, her fear exposed.

His expression lost all humour as he slid the tie from his neck and curled it, as if it were a snake, on the bed. She almost died when his hands went to the buckle on his belt. 'I don't think you should adopt that superior tone with me,' he warned, then whipped the belt out from his trousers, snapping it in front of her before it too joined the tie. 'It doesn't bring out the best in me.' He shrugged out of his jacket and threw it away, then began on the buttons of his shirt.

'You can't seriously mean to do this,' she rasped, terror a vice in her chest.

'To do what?' he smiled.

'To. . . to assault me.'

'Assault?' He feigned mock-surprise, and pulled off his shirt. Salome was shocked to see

that, although overweight, he looked amazingly
strong, his chest and shoulders massive. 'I have
no intention of assaulting you, my dear. Once
you're suitably subdued and...restrained...I'll
make sure you enjoy it. In fact, I'll guarantee it.
After all, I know what you are. I know where
you come from. You've learnt to put on airs and
graces, but, underneath the designer clothes and
ladylike veneer, you're nothing but a slut, like
your mother.' He picked up the belt and began
moving towards her, an evil, thin-lipped smile
beneath his equally thin moustache. 'God, I'm
going to enjoy this!' he breathed. 'I've been
wanting to do it for years!'

Salome moved with a strength and speed she
didn't realise she had. But her adrenalin was high,
panic and desperation inspiring her to attempt
anything in her own defence. Snatching the heavy
brass bedside lamp into shaking hands, she reared
up to crash it down on to her assailant's head
before he knew what was happening. Groaning,
he collapsed over the bed then began sliding down
on to the floor.

She didn't wait to see what the damage was.
Scrambling from the bed, she snatched up a towel
from a chair and raced from the room, wrapping
the towel around her naked body. Within seconds she was out in the corridor, where she fled
along and began hammering on Mike's door,
pounding and screaming for him to help her.

He couldn't have been asleep, for the door was
flung open almost immediately, and he was
standing there in a maroon dressing-gown.
Startled black eyes swept over her. 'Salome! What

on earth's going on? Hell, you haven't got any
damned clothes on! Here...put this on.'

He swept off his dressing-gown and helped her
flustered body into it, leaving him with only the
bottom half of navy silk pyjamas and a magni-
ficently bare chest. It was a tribute to Salome's
fear and consternation that she hardly noticed.

'Oh, God!' she sobbed again, letting the towel
drop as she sashed the gown tightly around her
like a shield. 'I hit him. I might have killed him!'

'Hit who? Killed who?'

'Oh, don't ask me questions. Just come!' she
cried, grabbing one of his arms with wildly trembling hands, and tugging him out into the
corridor.

'All right, all right.'

He followed her back into the other penthouse, where Salome stopped at the doorway to
the bedroom, shaking and pointing. 'In
there . . . beside the bed . . . Charles
Smeaton...Ralph's lawyer...'

Mike flashed her a look that suggested he
couldn't believe what he was hearing. 'You had
a *man* up here? Tonight? *After* you left me?'

For a second she didn't comprehend what he
was getting at. But then she groaned, understanding dawning like a winter's day, bleak and
cold. 'No, no, it's not what you think.' She shook
her head dejectedly. Oh, God, it was so typical
of him to believe the worst of her. Typical and
despicably predictable. Her dismay eventually
found voice in strangled, desolate words. 'I was
alone...asleep. I woke to find Charles in my
room. He——'

'How did he get in?' Mike interrupted, frowning darkly.

Salome's sigh was despairing. Did he have to sound so disbelieving? 'Charles obviously had a duplicate set of keys,' she explained frustratedly. 'It was he who handed me over my keys earlier today. I suppose he used the private basement elevator to avoid the security man in the foyer.'

'Mm.' Mike still looked sceptical. 'So what happened next?'

'He was staring at me in bed, and then he came in and started undressing. He——' She broke off, the memory of her near-escape sweeping over her, bringing nausea and a feeling of faintness. She swayed, and Mike caught her by her upper arms, his eyes rounding with what looked like horror.

'He didn't rape you, did he?'

She heaved in a shuddering breath. 'No...but he was going to. I...I asked him to leave, but he wouldn't. I was in bed, you see, and I couldn't get out. I...I didn't have any clothes on. He took off his belt, and...' Another shudder reverberated through her. 'I think he was going to beat me first,' she husked. 'He——' Her voice died, cut off by the appalled and incredulous expression on Mike's face.

She smothered a sob of utter despair. 'It's true!' she cried. 'As God is my witness, it's true.'

For what seemed like ages he just stared at her, and then his eyes saddened with a type of weary resignation. 'I believe you, Salome,' he sighed, his hands lifting to rake back his hair with exasperated fingers. 'Truly...I believe you.'

His declaration of belief gave her cold comfort, for his words had a sardonic, bitter flavour that implied she was still at fault, as though somehow she inspired men to commit atrocities. Any indignation was swiftly followed by guilt, though, as she recalled what had happened in the lift, how she had eagerly welcomed his attentions, then spurned him later. A shamed heat burnt in her cheeks and her eyes dropped in dismay. How could she blame him for thinking what he did? She had indeed acted like the tease he'd accused her of always being.

Thinking about what had happened between them in the lift, however, did not produce a guilty reaction for long. Instead, it flooded her mind with memories and her body with feelings that were very distracting, especially with Mike standing so close to her in his half-naked state.

Her gaze slowly lifted to flick over him, lingering far too long on the tanned breadth of his shoulders and chest, the smattering of dark curls running from below his throat down to his navel, exposed by the rather low-slung pyjama-trousers.

The sound of a groan coming from the bedroom had Salome's eyes flying away from their perturbing travels to where two unsteady hands were appearing over the side of the bed, clutching at the sheet. Her heart somersaulted. Good grief, she had virtually forgotten all about Charles, her mind having been totally consumed by her escalating feelings for the man in front of her!

But, with her assailant actually getting to his feet, fear renewed itself in a painfully constricted chest. Charles was a big man, even bigger than Mike, who was at present moving into the bedroom, leaving Salome clutching at the door-frame, her eyes big and frightened.

Charles finally stood up, holding the side of his head. He threw Salome a vicious glare. 'You bitch!' he snarled, and made a jagged lunge forwards before suddenly seeing Mike standing on the other side of the bed. He was momentarily taken aback, wobbling on unsteady feet. But then he straightened, his mouth twisting in an ugly and aggressive fashion.

'Called in the cavalry, did she? Well, it won't do her any good. I'll have that bitch in court for assault. I never touched her, you know,' he flung at Mike. 'If she says I did, she's a liar. All I wanted to do was talk!'

'You take off your shirt to talk?' came the drawled comment from Mike.

Charles's blood-shot eyes blinked, his legal mind slowly ticking over. His moustache thinned further as his lips drew back in a smug smile. 'So we were going to do more than talk. So what? Believe me, bud, she invited me in here. You don't see any signs of a forced entry, do you?'

'Nice try,' Mike rejoined. 'Too bad about the illegally kept set of keys in your pocket.'

Guilt was written all over Charles's face, but he tried to bluff his way out of it with a snarled, 'She gave them to me.'

Salome's eyes raced to Mike. She was aston-ished at how unconcerned he looked as he moved

around the foot of the bed to stand between
Charles and herself, his arms folding in a nonchalant but confident fashion.

'Who the bloody hell are you, anyway?'
Charles jeered. 'Some fancy playboy neighbour
she's sucking up to already?'

'Your judge and jury,' Mike said in a low,
steady voice.

Charles looked taken aback for a second, then
aggressive. He squared his shoulders, his wide-
legged stance very threatening. 'Don't bite off
more than you can chew, pretty boy. I was quite
a boxer in my day.'

'I'm terrified,' Mike drawled, giving his op-
ponent a dismissive glance.

Charles's face went red with fury. 'Cocky
bastard, aren't you? Well, cop this!' His fist shot
out quickly, but Mike was quicker, side-stepping
and grabbing Charles's arm, twisting it round
behind his back, then pushing him face-down on
to the bed, his knee jamming down in the small
of the lawyer's back. Charles began making
smothered groaning sounds.

Mike held him there while he looked up at a
wide-eyed, breathless Salome with amazing
nonchalance.

'Be a good girl and go and put some coffee
on, will you?' he suggested mildly. 'I'll be out to
have it after your friend and I have had a little
chat. He seems to be labouring under the most
peculiar misconceptions about justice.'

'Yes, but——'

'Not now, Salome,' he broke in firmly. 'Later.
Close the door and go.'

She closed the door. But she didn't go.

She stood staring at the door for some time, amazed and undeniably impressed. She had never witnessed such a devastating display of macho skill and strength, and she felt quite overwhelmed by it all. Who would ever have guessed that Mike's polished and gentlemanly façade hid such a powerful, primitive streak?

A shiver raced up and down her spine at the realisation that such a man would stop at nothing to get his own way, particularly with the weaker sex. This thought should have struck dread into her heart, yet her only response was an upsurge in sexual excitement. Now she wanted him more than ever!

She shook her head, disgusted with herself. What was the matter with her? Hadn't she learnt from her mother's mistakes? Heavens, she'd spent her entire life seeing the end result of relationships based on sex and sex alone! Which was all she'd ever have with Mike. The man didn't like or respect her. He merely wanted her. To even contemplate an affair with him was crazy!

Salome sighed crossly, turning to march across to the kitchen, where it took her ages to find the coffee-percolator and the essentials to make the ordered coffee, telling herself that if she weren't indebted to Sir Galahad for flattening Charles she wouldn't be making him any damn thing.

'Not that Sir Galahad is a good description,' she grumbled aloud as she shoved the plug into the power-point. 'More like the Black Knight, come to *ravage* the fair damsel in distress rather than *rescue* her!'

Several minutes later, the coffee-machine was perking away, its tantalising aroma teasing her nostrils, when the main bedroom door opened and Mike came out, leading a white-faced and oddly dressed Charles. The jacket and tie looked incongruous over his bare chest, his shirt still out in the hall.

The beady grey eyes didn't even glance her way as he was shepherded through the living area towards the front door. He looked amazingly cowered, and seemed to have shrunk a few inches.

Salome watched the silent procession in awe, wondering what Mike had said or done to achieve such a transformation in her assailant, from blustering bully to total coward in ten minutes. Charles looked sick, but he didn't look as if he'd been hit. Besides, she surely would have heard the sounds of a further beating?

'Goodnight, Charles,' Mike said equably as he opened the door. 'I sincerely hope it won't be necessary for us to meet again.'

Charles looked even sicker at this, if that were possible, and stumbled out the door.

Mike closed it with a quiet click, turning to walk slowly over to Salome. It flustered and annoyed her the way her heart stepped up its beat as he approached, not to mention the way she kept staring at him. She tried focusing her mind on her divorce and the pain it had caused, thinking that that would sway her from any further disastrous involvements with selfishly motivated males.

But no... her pulse-rate kept doing a jig, and an uncomfortable heat started sweeping across her skin as he drew closer and closer, his dark eyes both assessing and speculative.

At the critical moment she spun away and hurried behind the breakfast-bar, busying herself organising cups and saucers, chattering away to cover the rattling of her shaking hands.

'I don't know how to thank you enough,' she said, 'or how you managed to subdue Charles so totally. He really scared me, you know, though I do think he was quite drunk, and maybe he wouldn't have done anything; but who knows?' She shrugged and threw Mike a nervous glance. He was staring at her across the counter with hard, unfathomable eyes, and she would have given anything to know what he was thinking.

But she suspected he would never tell her, and to keep staring back would be to reveal what she herself was thinking: that he was quite marvellously male and virile and gorgeous and, oh, dear God, she wanted him like crazy!

So she dragged her eyes back to what she was doing quite ineptly, spilling some milk on the counter-top as she transferred it from carton to cup. 'I'm afraid there was only long-life milk in the cupboards,' she rattled on. 'You take milk in your coffee, don't you? You did at the restaurant tonight.'

She was about to pick up the percolator to pour when firm hands closed over her shoulders. Her fingers froze mid-air, and she gasped as Mike pulled her back against him.

'I don't really want coffee,' he murmured at her ear.

Slowly he turned her round, and Salome found herself looking into eyes that told a million stories, all with the same ending. 'I merely said that to give you something to do,' he soothed. 'You were looking lost.'

Salome swallowed. 'Lost'... What a good word. Yes, that was what she definitely was. Lost... When her marriage had ended she'd been tossed out on to an aimless sea, a ship without a rudder, floating aimlessly, a virtual wreck.

But the man holding her captive and looking down into her eyes was no real salvager, merely one of those scrap-metal dealers who took dead ships to their grave, stripping them of all they were worth and leaving their ghastly empty hulls to rust and ruin.

Her graphic thoughts sent renewed panic into her heart, and she would have pulled back if his grip hadn't tightened at that moment. She flinched under his bruising hold. 'What is it you want, then?' she choked out.

His smile was strangely sad. 'The same thing I've always wanted, Salome. You...'

She stared up at him, unable to understand why he wanted her when he despised her so. Was it just an answer to the challenge he thought she had thrown out to him all those years ago? Or was she always to be plagued with men who only desired her? 'I—I can't,' she blurted out in fear of what would become of her if she gave in.

'Why not?' he persisted. 'You want to. Our encounter in the lift proved that. Besides, I saw it in your eyes a few minutes ago. The need, the yearning. You're lonely, Salome. Lonely and alone. Let me be with you tonight, to make love to you, comfort you.'

It all sounded so reasonable. And he wasn't even dressing it up with false words of love.

She stared at him with a mixture of desire and wariness, mindful that he had changed tack on her somewhere, substituting the masterful macho play with a more seductive, subtle tactic. And it was working, too, slipping past her defences to make her melt inside. The temptation to lean against his bare chest, to give herself up to his will, was overwhelming. A low moan escaped her lips before she could smother it. And then it was too late, her head moving of its own accord to nestle into his warm brown throat, a sigh of surrender wafting from deep within her breast.

Mike didn't say a word. He merely swept her up into his arms and carried her from the penthouse, down the hall, and into his own place, kicking the door shut behind him. Only then did he look into her eyes, shocking her with the violence of emotion burning in their black depths.

'If you change your mind again,' he warned darkly, 'I'm likely to strangle you!'

With that, he continued on into the bedroom, once again kicking the door shut behind him.

CHAPTER SEVEN

I CAN'T possibly be doing this, Salome thought
as Mike laid her down on a bed in the dark. When
he snapped on a bedside lamp, her eyes darted
nervously around the dimly lit room, which was
as exquisitely and blandly furnished as Ralph's
main bedroom, and just as impersonal. Not a
photograph or a memento in sight. Her eyes returned to the man who was now sitting on the
side of the king-size bed, watching her with a
closed expression on his face. And it came to her
that he was virtually a stranger.

What did she know of him? Only that he was
in his early thirties, unmarried, lived here in this
penthouse, and owned an Italian restaurant.
Everything else she'd gleaned about him had been
sheer gossip or speculation.

Their conversation over dinner the evening
before had been desultory to say the least, betraying nothing of his background or his private
life. For all she knew he could be part of that
network of Italian immigrants whose businesses
were merely fronts for organised crime. Drug-
running and the like. His restaurant *was* in King's
Cross, after all—the crime centre of Sydney. She
had read of such men—men who made and lived
by their own rules. Powerful, ruthless men.

The image of a white-faced Charles giving
Mike a sick look jumped into her mind, and her

stomach turned over. Good God, surely he couldn't be a member of the Mafia?

Much as she immediately rejected that idea as one of an over-active imagination, her thoughts had alarmed her, making her want to jump up from the bed and run for her very life. But she lay there, stiff with expectation and apprehension.

'You're nervous,' he said, almost accusingly.

She gulped down the lump in her throat and turned her face away from those probing black eyes. His hand closed over her chin and turned her back, where she was astonished to see a wry smile on his lips. 'They say women are hard to understand,' he murmured, his thumb moving in soft, tantalising circles along her jawline. 'But you, my lovely Salome, are the hardest of them all.'

He bent and covered her mouth with his, moving his lips back and forth across hers with slow, unhurried movements. She sucked in a startled breath as the most incredible wave of delight rippled through her. His head lifted a few inches, his eyes revealing a measure of surprise. 'You're amazing,' he whispered. 'If I didn't know better, I'd say this was your first time...'

He kissed her again, this time teasing her mouth open and caressing the tip of her tongue with his. Desire seized Salome in its tenacious grip, making her moan deep in her throat.

Again Mike straightened to gaze frustratedly at the dazed expression on her face. 'I can see why men go crazy for you,' he muttered, his fingers drifting down her throat to trace the 'V' of the dressing-gown, making her shiver when he lingered on the valley between her breasts. 'You are whatever they want of you at the time. In the lift, a wild wanton, here, a virgin on her wedding night, tentative and sweet, amazed yet delighted by your responses. How do you do it, Salome?' he said, half admiringly, half derisively. 'How many years of practice did it take to master the fine art of erotic fantasy?'

There was no time for an answer, even if her hurt mind could have thought of one. His mouth swooped to claim hers again, and this time it was hungry and demanding, his lips applying a bruising pressure, his tongue thrusting deep into her mouth, pushing aside her renewed dismay, leaving room for little but the crazed leap in her senses.

'God!' he muttered when at last he tore his mouth away, smouldering black eyes locking on to stunned green ones. Salome gave a soft whimper when his fingertips moved across her dark, swollen lips. 'I'm sorry,' he rasped. 'I'm not usually so brutal.'

'Don't be sorry,' she said huskily. 'I liked it.'

Liked it? What an outrageous under-statement! She'd loved it, adored it, *ached* for it! She could think of nothing more exciting than having this man ravishing her.

Aroused eyes lifted to run up one of the strong male arms that imprisoned her, landing on his broad bare chest. The desire to touch the taut, finely honed muscles was overpowering, her right hand lifting to trail a tentative but sensuous path across his skin, her nails raking lightly over one of his male nipples.

The intensity of his shudder surprised her, as did the heat of the flesh beneath her fingers. With a rush of raw, mindless passion, she wrapped both her arms around his waist and pulled herself up till her face was pressed against his chest, opening moist lips on to his skin, sliding them across the hot, hard wall of muscle till it closed over where her nails had just been.

He shuddered again, then groaned as her tongue darted forward to tease the hard nub, encircling it slowly then nipping it with her teeth as he had done to her in the lift. Suddenly, strong hands grabbed her shoulders and pushed her away from him. 'You must stop,' he rasped. 'Stop!'

She stared at him in confusion, her heart pounding madly. What had she done wrong?

'I think you'd better revert to the shy virgin,' he growled, letting her go to run agitated hands through his hair.

Salome cringed visibly, thinking she had just made a dreadful fool of herself.

'God, woman, don't look like that! Do you think I wasn't enjoying it? Hell, I was enjoying it too much. The truth is, I haven't had sex in bloody ages and, if you keep that up, this'll be all over before it damned well starts!'

Salome stared at him, shocked at how much his confession of recent celibacy pleased her. But then came the cynical realisation that, for a virile man like him, a *fortnight* was probably ages. She glanced around at the huge bed with its cream satin sheets and myriad pillows, and she knew with absolute certainty that many women had been here before her, had lain eagerly beneath his gorgeous male body, had accepted his hungry kisses, had been thrilled by his overt sexuality.

Her jealousy was instant and savage, cutting a sharp path through her chest up into her brain. Her eyes snapped back up to him, and she wanted to tear his beautiful face apart, wanted to scream at him that he was never to make love to another woman ever again. That he was hers from this night forward. Hers and hers alone!

The intensity, the insanity of her feelings shook her. Surely this couldn't be just normal sexual frustration she was suffering from? This was something far deeper, far more devastating.

'What is it?' Mike said sharply.

She expelled the breath she had been holding in a trembling gasp. 'Nothing...nothing...'

'Tell me,' he urged, and drew her to him in a breathtakingly close embrace, his lips pressed feverishly to her forehead. 'What is it that frightens you so about me? Why didn't you want to let me finish making love to you earlier on? *Why?*'

She shook her head frantically from side to side. 'I don't want to talk about it,' she whispered hoarsely. 'I can't! It's all too confusing.'

'What's confusing?' he insisted, little knowing that the hot, stroking hands on her hair, her neck, her back, were the most confusing of all, because they kept bringing wave after wave of sensation that was slowly obliterating her capacity to reason. Surely she wouldn't feel like this in any other man's arms, would she? It didn't seem possible. Yet . . . if it was only Michael Angellini who could do this to her, then what was it exactly she felt for him? Sexual infatuation? Obsession? Lust?

Salome refused to embrace the word 'love'. Even if her feelings for Ralph had finally begun to die, her bruised, battered heart wasn't ready, or capable, of loving another man yet, and certainly not a man who had nothing but contempt for her. Perhaps she was acting this way out of some sort of crazed revenge against the hurt perpetrated by her husband. Perhaps this was a rebound thing. She didn't know any more.

'Everything's confusing,' she groaned. 'Me . . . this . . . you . . .'

His fingers stilled abruptly. 'What do you mean?'

She freed herself from his frozen grip, looking up at him with bleak green eyes. 'I don't know! Can't you see I don't really know anything any more? It's all been too much for me today. First Ralph, then Charles, now you. I'm so mixed up!' she cried, and covered her distressed face with her hands.

'You want me to stop,' he said in a dead, flat voice.

Her head snapped up and her eyes flew to him, wild, wild eyes. 'No,' she groaned. 'That's the most confusing part. I don't.'

His eyes raked over her, from her turbulent gaze to her parted, quivering lips to the way her breasts were rising and falling beneath the dressing-gown.

'I couldn't anyway,' he rasped. 'Not even if I wanted to.'

In an electric silence his hands lifted to find the pins in her hair, throwing them away before returning to spread her tumbling mass of curls out across her shoulders. Then slowly—ever so slowly—he untied the sash of the dressing-gown and parted it, peeling it back across her shoulders and down her arms to drop on to the sheet.

Salome scooped in a breath and held it. Don't think any more, she told herself. Don't think. Close your eyes and just feel!

She expelled a shuddering sigh as she obeyed her own instructions, closing her eyes and waiting breathlessly for the moment when he would start touching her breasts. They were infinitely ready for him. Swollen and taut, her nipples still erect and sensitised from his earlier lovemaking in the lift.

'Oh!' she gasped when something hard and warm grazed over both tips at once. Her lashes fluttered open to reveal outstretched palms rubbing over them in slow, sensuous circles. His eyes were on hers, watching her with a heavy-lidded, smouldering gaze. Then he was caressing her whole breasts, cupping their soft weight in his hands, kneading them, lifting them, pushing them together, bending his mouth to one after the other.

Her head fell backwards in automatic abandon, the riotous bronze curls spilling from her neck. She pressed closed fists down into the mattress, thrusting her breasts upwards into those intoxicating hands, that tormenting mouth. Soft moans of arousal floated from her throat.

He lowered her to the bed and just looked at her. She looked back in a dazed rapture. 'You are the most beautiful, the most sensual, the most responsive woman I have ever known,' he murmured, and resumed stroking her body, making her gasp as he ran light fingers across her aching nipples once more. 'I could drown in your eyes when they look like that. And your mouth...' He groaned and bent to take her parted lips in a deep, hungry kiss, one hand scooping under her neck to hold her mouth firmly captive beneath his, the other sliding over her flat stomach, down between her thighs, where he began a shockingly intimate exploration of her body.

Salome was overwhelmed by the violently pleasurable sensations and feelings that besieged her with the liberties he was taking. They frightened her. This couldn't be how lovemaking was supposed to feel, she thought frantically. Not this crazed, escalating need, this mad desire to submit to *anything*!

'No more!' she gasped when he finally abandoned her mouth. But any relief was short-lived as he began trailing hot, moist lips down her body, bypassing her breasts in a direct route towards that part of her body that was already on fire.

A tortured moan punched from her throat when she realised what he was about to do. And while the thought of it excited her unbearably, she knew she wouldn't be able to stand it. But there was no stopping him, his hands masterful and dominating as they parted her thighs, his mouth insistently possessive as it moved over her in the ultimate intimacy.

She was right. She couldn't stand it, the blisteringly electric sensations making her cry out. He totally ignored her whimpering moans, her hands fluttering in feeble protest in his hair, and continued his devastating attentions with an expertise that was both telling and breathtakingly hypnotic. Here was a man who not only knew all there was to know about women, but who wasn't prepared to take no for an answer, a man who could destroy her even more thoroughly than Ralph had.

But there was no room for regrets or future concerns at such a moment. Salome was beyond that, caught up in a journey of erotic pleasure from which there was no turning back. Tighter and tighter her body felt, faster and faster her breathing, hotter and hotter her blood. She was being swept up a previously unknown mountain, racing towards a peak from which there could be only one way down. And, even though the prospect of experiencing what she had never experienced before was intoxicatingly compulsive, suddenly Salome knew she didn't want it this way, couldn't *bear* it this way. She wanted Mike inside her, *needed* Mike inside her.

She moaned her frustration and frantically pushed him away, 'No, no!' she cried.

He staggered back off the end of the bed, getting to his feet and staring down at her with eyes both wild and incredulous. 'You must be mad! There's no stopping now. No changing your mind. Look at me!' And, with a single savage yank, he stripped off his pyjama-trousers, striking her speechless with the stark evidence of his desire.

Salome had never looked quite so blatantly at an aroused man before, certainly not one as well-endowed as Mike. Colour burnt in her cheeks, her heart thudding beneath her breasts. 'I haven't changed my mind,' she burst forth, then hesitated, finding it hard to find the words. 'I was wanting you. *You!*' she cried. 'Not... anything less...'

His groan was tortured, his eyes squeezing tightly shut for a second. But then he was shaking his head and sinking back down on top of her, the anger punching from his lungs in a ragged sigh. 'Then why didn't you say so? Dear God, I thought——'

Again he groaned, then knelt upright to run shaking hands over her body, easing her thighs apart. Her eyes grew wide, her heart stopping as he scooped his hands under her buttocks and lifted her to meet him. She felt his flesh, hard against her softness, and then he was sinking into her, filling the aching void, taking her breath away. She moaned her pleasure as her body encompassed the entire length of him, her hands reaching up to drag him down to her waiting warmth.

This was how making love was meant to feel, she cried silently, two people as one, man and woman as nature had intended.

His mouth sought hers again as he began to move, slowly, rhythmically, deeply. Waves of pleasure—both emotional and physical—pervaded Salome's body and senses, making her block out all thought of Mike being no more than a womaniser with no real caring for her. Right here, tonight, he was the man she wanted above all others; he was *her* man. He had just shown her how much he wanted her and, for now, it had to be enough.

Tomorrow she would probably despair over what she was doing now. More than probably. Yet somehow she was unable to summon any regret at this moment. All she knew was how marvellous it felt to be joined with Mike like this. Marvellous and exciting and overwhelming.

Finally he gasped away from her mouth and pressed hot lips to the smooth skin of her shoulder, the pulsating vein at the base of her throat, his hands running up and down the sides of her body. Her own hands were caressing the muscles in his back, but dug sharply inwards when he grabbed her hips, lifting them from the bed and thrusting even more deeply into her. Quite instinctively, her inner muscles squeezed tightly around his throbbing hardness, gripping and releasing him in a relentless rhythm. Any moment now...

There was a split second when she seemed to balance on a sharp edge, when her breathing stopped, and every muscle in her body strained to an aching stop. She heard him gasp for breath, felt his hands tightening around her. Then, with one final surge, he set them both free, and their mutual cries of release echoed in the night.

Salome was stunned, not only by the intensity of her physical feelings, but also by her emotional ones. She hugged Mike's shuddering body to her till it stilled, unable to stop a crazed litany from tumbling through her mind.

I love him . . . I love him . . . I love him . . .

She grimaced in denial of it, knowing in her brain that it wasn't true, and hating herself for the way her heart kept wanting to embrace the idea. This was lust, not love. Sexual satisfaction, not spiritual bonding. A one-night stand, not their wedding night.

But try as she might to dampen her joy with ruthless reasoning, she couldn't. She felt wonderfully at peace, and very, very happy.

'Oh, Mike,' she sighed, raining kisses across his chest. 'I want to stay like this forever.'

Sensual black eyes stared down at her, a languorous smile coming to his mouth. Salome wondered if her own lips looked as wonderfully ravaged as his. 'Happy to oblige,' he drawled. 'When are you going to move in with me?'

She gasped her surprise. Of all things, she wasn't expecting this. 'You . . . you want me to live with you?'

'Either that or you give me a key to your place. I certainly want to spend my nights with you.' He leaned on both elbows either side of her. 'I want you, Salome,' he said with a strange undercurrent of urgency. 'Not just for one night. I need much more of you than that.'

Her mind whirled. She could hardly think rationally, not with her body still joined to his, her senses still dazed with pleasure. 'No, Mike,

I can't!' she cried, before the insidious temptation to say yes overcame her.

'Don't put crazy arguments in the way!' he cut in, his hands intimidating as they captured her face. 'Your marriage to Ralph Diamond is past! Over! He doesn't want you any more. This is here...now. I want you and you want me.'

His eyes flashed angrily, his body quivering with suppressed rage as he tried to control himself. 'Why do you keep finding ways to deny me what you've given others? Hell, Salome, you've been driving me mad for years. I've thought of nothing else but having you, possessing you. I'm mad about you, woman, can't you see that?'

His kiss was savage, yet oddly desperate. And it was the desperation that moved Salome more than the seductive skill of his lips and tongue.

'Say you'll be mine,' he urged when the kiss was over and he had successfully reduced her to a panting, mindless mass.

'Yes,' she said, breathlessly, blindly. 'Yes...'

'You won't say no to me ever again,' he rasped, his eyes glittering with triumph. His mouth descended once more, his hands hard and exciting on her body, sweeping Salome along with his rapidly renewed passion.

His words were prophetic, at least where the next few hours were concerned. He made love to Salome in ways she had never been made love to before, demanding things she had never freely given before, each experience showing her there were sexual horizons still to be explored, pla-

teaus of pleasure not yet reached, surrenders she
had never even envisaged.

Sunlight filtered through the curtains behind the
bed, landing in Salome's eyes and stirring her to
semi-consciousness. She sighed and rolled over,
one limp arm encountering a wall of warm flesh.
She froze, then pulled her arm back as instant
memories of the night before flooded in, startling
her to full awareness. Her eyes flew open.

Mike lay naked on his stomach, his face turned
away from her, his legs sprawled, his breathing
deep and even. She swallowed as her eyes followed the line of his spine, down between the
well-honed muscles of his back, down to where
she could see the red marks her nails had made
on his buttocks. Horrified, she glanced down at
her own nudity, green eyes widening at the be-
ginnings of bruises on her hips and thighs. Her
fingers trembled as they lifted to feel her raw,
puffy lips. Her tongue darted out to moisten
them, and she was certain she could still feel the
taste of him.

Smothering a groan, she carefully swung her
legs over the side of the bed, and levered herself
up on to her feet. With a slow, silent tread, she
made it across the plush white carpet into the
bathroom, locking the door behind her. A hot
bath beckoned, even though the tap running
might wake Mike. Still, the door was locked, so
he couldn't walk in on her—a thought that made
her shudder. How could she face him after all
she had done and allowed? Only the most wanton

women, she believed, acted as uninhibitedly as she had done.

With a disbelieving shake of her head, she found some bath gel in the well-appointed marble cabinet, then snapped on the gold taps. Soon she was lowering herself into the invitingly steaming waters. With a low moan, she lay back, and gradually the seeping heat soothed her stiffening body.

But not her troubled mind. What had she done, agreeing to be Mike's mistress? He didn't love her, despite the impassioned words he had rained on her during the night. And, much as she had fantasised she loved him in the throes of passion, in the cold light of day she knew she didn't. She had loved Ralph, and it had been nothing like this. It had never frightened her. It had felt safe and secure at the time, filled with warmth and light. This feeling, though, was dark and dangerous and destructive.

It was also very strong, much stronger than common sense or even shame. Already she wanted to feel what it was like to have his hands on her again, to experience that exquisitely electric release once more.

It was just as well, Salome realised with bitter irony, that she couldn't get pregnant. Though this was through sheer good luck rather than design, her doctor having recently put her on the Pill to regulate her periods. She did want to have children eventually, but only with a man who loved her.

A sharp knocking on the bathroom door had her jerking upright, her wet curls plastering down her back. 'You haven't drowned in there, have you, Salome?'

'No,' she called back, grateful that single words didn't sound shaky or nervous.

'Just checking. Don't be too long.'

His tone of voice sounded perfectly normal. Clearly, *he* wasn't bothered by the prospect of facing her this morning.

What a naïve fool you are, Salome, she berated herself, worrying about what he might think of you. Goodness, all you did was act exactly as he expected you to act, and as, no doubt, *all* his lovers act. Do you honestly believe you are the first woman to have surrendered herself so totally to his extraordinary sexual appetite? Of course not!

And for goodness' sake don't start believing all those crazy, glorious words he said to you about never having felt what he felt when he was with you. No doubt words of that ilk just fall from his mouth quite automatically whenever he makes love. What better way to make a woman come back for more, than by making her feel special and unique? The only difference between you and a host of others is that he's had to wait for you longer than most, which is probably why he seemed so desperate on occasions last night.

He doesn't love you. Did you notice how carefully he avoided saying that he did? Oh, yes, he wanted you, needed you, adored you, found you exciting and sexy and breathtakingly beautiful. But he never mentioned the word 'love'. So if you do this crazy thing and become his lover—and you're going to, aren't you?—then don't ever start fantasising that he does. Try to remember you are dealing with a Don Juan here!

Salome sighed and struggled out of the bath, wrapping her dripping hair in one of the huge fluffy cream towels, her body in another. She gave her teeth a thorough scrub with one of the spare toothbrushes lying in the top drawer, then straightened, turning away before she could catch a glimpse of herself in the mirror. She didn't want to look at herself, didn't want to hold in her memory the image of a woman who was about to do the most stupid, insane thing she had ever done in her entire life!

CHAPTER EIGHT

SALOME found a maroon-robed Mike in the kitchen, brewing even better-smelling coffee than she'd made the previous night. Its delicious aroma, however, ran a distant second where her senses were concerned. They were being filled with the man who was standing next to the percolator, tapping idle fingers on the marble counter-top. Obviously he had used the main bathroom to shower while she'd been in the en suite, for his hair was slicked back behind his ears in wet waves, the style giving her an unimpeded view of his very male profile with its strong, Roman nose and stubborn cleft chin. His mind seemed to be a million miles away, his furrowed brow indicating a serious train of thought.

He must have seen her suddenly out of the corner of his eye, for his head jerked round, his startled gaze raking over her towel-clad body, lingering on bare shoulders before dropping to her equally bare feet. For a moment it was as though he didn't recognise her, his eyes narrowing with a kind of disapproval as they swept back up to land on her freshly scrubbed face.

Salome's heart lurched, then sank. Apparently he preferred his women glammed up, even at breakfast.

He was shaking his head. 'You look about fifteen,' he said. His dry tone brought a spurt of anger, and she pulled the towel from around her head, letting the red-gold curls spill in damp disarray around her face and shoulders. She knew if anything could destroy the illusion of youthful innocence it was her wild mass of hair. 'Better?' she snapped.

His eyes raked over her again, and this time desire flared in those ruthless black pools. Salome was shocked. My God, hadn't he had enough last night? She tore her eyes away from him, alarmed that recognition of *his* desire had stirred her also. If this kept up they would spend all their *days* in bed, not just their nights!

A black wave of dismay rolled through her. What in heaven's name was she doing, wasting more of her life on another man who didn't love her? This was even worse than her marriage to Ralph. It didn't even have the respectability of a wedding-ring, or the illusion of love! If she had any guts she would walk out of here right now.

Her dismay grew, for she knew she couldn't do it. She wanted Mike too much. All she could hope for was that their affair would be a short one, that her mad desires would be sated before he succeeded in ensnaring more than her bodily responses. In her present vulnerable state, it was within the realms of possibility that she might really fall in love with him. And *that*, she could do without.

Irritation at her own weakness brought a surge of pride-filled resolve. Get a hold of yourself, woman! You're an independent adult, not a simpering idiot with no will of your own. *You* call the shots. *You* decide what will be done and when. Don't let another man turn you into a puppet on a string!

Feeling infinitely stronger, she lifted cool green eyes, giving a still staring Mike a sophisticated smile as she walked slowly over and settled herself on one of the stools. 'Pour me some of that coffee, will you, darling?' she said, draping the damp towel in her hand over the stool next to her. 'I need something to wake me up.'

He glared at her, clearly annoyed with her casual attitude; or was it the socially meaningless 'darling' that had irked him?

Too bad, her eyes projected back with savage indifference. If you want to have an affair with a woman whom you think has few moral scruples, Michael Angellini, then don't be put out when she acts like one. Or did you honestly expect her to be the complete fantasy, and pretend undying love as well?

Clenching his jaw, he swung his attention back to the coffee which he poured into two stoneware mugs. Salome got the impression he would have liked to throw hers right at her, but he didn't. Instead, he put it down in front of her with that cold smile and exaggerated politeness he'd always treated her with at his restaurant. A jug of milk and a basin of sugar were deposited with controlled movements, as was a spoon.

'Do you want some eggs to go with that?' he asked with his cold restaurateur voice. 'Or some toast?'

'Some toast would be nice,' she returned blandly.

Actually, she didn't want toast. She wanted to get the hell out of here. Inside, she still felt thoroughly ashamed of herself, not only for what had happened the previous night, but also for what she knew was going to happen again tonight, and many nights to come. She would never have believed she could become addicted to sex like this, but the least she could do was control her new-found desires as best she could and dissuade Mike from any idea he might be harbouring of a master-slave relationship. Which meant she would have to make a stand on certain matters before it was too late, before she fell more under this man's sexual power than she was already.

'Mike,' she began firmly before she could change her mind. His head snapped up from the toaster, eyes hard.

'About my moving in with you,' she went on, her chest tightening at the way his eyes hardened even further. 'I would rather stay in my own place. I . . . you said it would be all right with you if I gave you a key.'

He said nothing for several seconds, his glare a troubled mixture of fury and undeniable disappointment. This latter reaction evoked a dangerous weakness within Salome. Incredibly, she was tempted to change her mind, to tell him she would do whatever he wanted, that she would be here for him always, whenever and however he wished.

In the end this very same weakness was her salvation. My God, if this was how her amazing new sense of sexuality was going to make her feel, then it was doubly imperative that she keep her own place and her own counsel, that this affair be on *her* terms, not Mike's.

'On second thoughts,' she resumed, her voice firming again, 'I'd rather not give you a key either. All you have to do is knock and I'll let you in. After all...' she gave him one of her coolest looks '... if I'm not at home, there's no point in your coming in, is there?'

For a long time they just stared at each other, with Salome again crazily wanting to take back what she had just said. But it was what she began wanting Mike to do that disturbed her the most. She wanted him to sweep her into his arms and tell her not to be so silly, that he really loved her, cared about her, that he wanted to spend time with her, not just in bed but out, wanted to be her friend and companion, not just her lover.

These unexpected desires were so unbelievably strong that they made her head spin. If she wanted him to love her so much, did that mean that the awful had already happened—that she had already fallen for him?

Her gaze went to his broodingly handsome face, his beautiful hands, his impressively virile body, probably naked under the dressing-gown. But she didn't concentrate on any of these things. Instead, she thought of all she had ever felt for this man, right from their first meeting, when hot black eyes had clashed with cool green ones, and her whole world had tilted, never to be the same again. Could the intensity of her reaction to him back then be reasoned away by blaming it on a thwarted though superficial sexual desire?

She didn't think so, and, as the scales of self-deception fell from her eyes, something deep moved inside Salome, something as intrinsically emotional and binding as it was physical. There seemed to be no separating them, no matter what she did, and finally she had to accept the truth. Yes, she did love him. Perhaps, in a weird way, she always had.

Her reaction to this acceptance was a wild mixture of despair and relief. Despair that it made a mockery of what she had always thought she'd felt for Ralph. Yet relief that she hadn't fallen victim to some unexpectedly promiscuous change in her nature. What more natural than to want to make love to the man she loved?

And it was while she was battling with a new rush of weakness towards him that Mike spoke up. 'Whatever you're comfortable with, Salome,' he agreed curtly.

She silenced the crazy words of confessed love that kept bubbling up in her throat by drinking down the scalding coffee and talking to herself. Don't you dare tell him, you silly little fool, she repeated over and over again. Ten minutes later she had gobbled down the toast and was excusing herself.

'I must go, Mike. Your kitchen clock says it's after ten. The day will be over before you know it, and I promised Molly I'd visit. Besides, I've many more things to bring over.'

He wasn't going to let her go that easily, however, and he walked her along the corridor to her still-open door, where he drew her into his arms, his cold eyes warming irresistibly when she made no moves to stop him. Salome found it impossible to concentrate on any resolves for her survival when he looked at her like that, particularly now that she knew she loved him.

Yet, this knowledge should have been making her more wary, more careful. If she had any sense she would put a halt to this right now, do what she'd decided to do yesterday and move back home.

'You're an intriguing woman, Salome,' he murmured. 'A woman of many colours. A chameleon. I thought I knew you, but I haven't touched the surface, have I?'

It took every ounce of her control to keep a cool and somewhat mysterious smile on her face. If she let him inside her head and her heart, she would be truly lost.

'I am what I am,' she said cryptically.

'Mm . . . and that's very sexy.' He bent to kiss her mouth lightly with his, teasing it with the tip of his tongue. 'I have to work tonight,' he whispered into her parting lips. 'It'll be late by the time I get in.'

'I'll wait up,' she returned shakily.

'I was hoping you'd say that.' His mouth completed what it had started, her acceptance of loving him giving the experience a poignant edge. It seemed to pierce into her very soul, making her want to cling to him, never to let him go. Her arms shot up around his neck, and she pulled him to her, returning his kiss with sudden blind urgency. He responded accordingly, his arms tightening around her, his hunger inflamed. But when he urged her inside her penthouse, and tried to remove the towel from around her, she wrenched herself away.

'No!' she cried, panic-stricken. 'No,' she repeated, with a shaky, apologetic smile, hoping it would waylay his troubled astonishment. 'There isn't time, darling. Sorry...I'll make it up to you tonight.' Clutching the dangerously drooping towel around her, she went up on tiptoe and gave him a dismissive peck.

He stared back down at her, not totally mollified. 'I wish I knew what went on inside that gorgeous head of yours,' he growled.

She laughed. 'What would be the fun in that?'

His face darkened with ill-humour. 'Who said this is fun? More like bloody torture!'

Salome blushed guiltily, knowing that her burst of love had unwittingly aroused him.

'And now she blushes,' he grated out. 'God!' He whirled around and stalked out into the corridor, where he seemed to have second thoughts, spinning round to throw her an exasperated though forgiving look. 'By the way, I'll see the janitor later about having the locks changed on your door and the basement lift,' he said. 'And I'll find out if we're likely to have any more of those blackouts. Hopefully, it was a one-off thing.'

Salome's stomach tightened as she thought of what had happened in the lift. Even her acceptance of loving Mike didn't stop the automatic feeling of shame.

Mike made a disgruntled sound, as though he too was remembering something best forgotten.

'I guess I'll see you later tonight,' he bit out in clipped tones, and stalked off.

'I guess so. . .' She closed the door and leaned against it, letting out a shuddering sigh. A whole day without him, she thought. And despite all her resolves, all her common-sense reasonings, her heart plummeted. 'How am I going to stand it?' she groaned to the cold, empty rooms.

CHAPTER NINE

WALKING into the bedroom and seeing the brass lamp lying on the floor beside the rumpled bed sent a chill through Salome. What would have happened if she had missed, if Charles had overpowered her, or if Mike hadn't been next door to come to the rescue? She slumped down on the end of the bed and dropped her head into her hands, feeling unexpectedly nauseous.

Mike was right to get the locks changed. Charles still had his set of keys. What was to stop him sneaking back some time, perhaps when Mike was out? The thought sent shivers up and down her spine, and she reminded herself always to put the chain across and also to buy one of those alarms which women could use to frighten off an assailant.

Salome sighed and straightened, feeling better with her resolves. She had never been a physical coward, and she wasn't about to start now.

Less than an hour later the bedroom was tidied, the stale coffee in the percolator poured away, the towel around her replaced by a tailored pair of khaki trousers and a cowl-necked lemon mohair jumper, her hair tied back with a lemon ribbon. Her make-up was at a minimum. Grey-green eye-shadow, mascara and coral lipstick. No foundation or blusher. The lengthy bath had put a healthy glow in her normally pale cheeks.

With tan loafers on her feet and a matching bag slung over her shoulder, she fairly dashed along the corridor, then started the long trek down the fire-stairs, determined not to go in that lift again till she'd been assured it wouldn't break down. Hopefully, this would be by the time she needed to go back up!

The first thing she saw when she stepped out into the basement car park was Mike, standing behind her Ferrari with his hands on his hips. If she hadn't been so taken aback by his clothing she might have noticed that he was staring down at something, his face grim. As it was, all her attention was riveted to his tight, stone-washed grey jeans, white T-shirt and black leather flying-jacket.

She smothered a groan. Wasn't he sexy enough, without dressing like Marlon Brando in *The Wild One*? And what in heaven was he doing down here anyway?

He glanced up at her as she approached, his expression turning to one of open admiration as it flicked over this more softly casual though still stylish version of herself. It was when his dark brows suddenly bunched together in a black frown and he glared back down at the car that she realised something was wrong.

'What is it?' she said, hurrying forward. She followed his downward glance with her own. The Ferrari was low on the cement, all four tyres viciously slashed. 'Oh, no...'

'It's easily fixable,' he assured her.

She grimaced, then frowned up at him. 'Charles, do you think?'

'Perhaps. Perhaps not. It could have been the gang of kids who apparently sabotaged the main fuse-box with fire-crackers last night. Hence the blackout.'

'Oh...' Salome hoped it was. The image of Charles doing anything as vindictive as this was frightening. Mike wasn't looking too happy about it either.

'I think, Salome,' he began firmly, 'that we should drop in on your ex-husband and tell him what his lawyer's been up to.'

She panicked at the idea. She no longer wanted to see Ralph. She certainly wasn't up to facing him today. 'That's impossible,' she said hastily. 'He... he won't see anyone.'

'He'll see me.'

Salome stared at his supremely confident face, and didn't doubt it. There was a force in Mike that could be quite unstoppable once on the move.

'He... he has cameras on top of the gates,' she went on nervously. 'If he sees me with you, he won't let you in, believe me.'

'Then he won't see you with me,' he stated unequivocally. 'You can duck down.'

What could she say? She had gone on and on to Mike just yesterday about all the times she had tried to see Ralph. Now here he was, giving her the perfect opportunity to confront her ex-husband with moral support at her side, and she didn't want to take it. What was she so frightened of finding out? She already knew about the other woman.

She shook her head in frustrated resignation. 'Oh, all right. But don't say I didn't warn you. Once Ralph finds out we've tricked him, he'll throw us out.'

'He wouldn't want to try,' Mike said darkly.

Salome shivered. There was something about Mike that frightened her at times, an air of suppressed violence. Was it this quality that had cowered Charles so devastatingly? Or had she been right when she'd wondered if Mike had an unsavoury background?

'Mike...' she began gingerly.

He glanced up from where he'd been looking at the tyres again. 'What?'

She swallowed. 'What did you do to Charles last night? What did you say to make him back down? I couldn't believe it when he came out looking so...so defeated.'

A wry smile lifted the corner of his mouth. 'There's no great secret. I merely pointed out what might happen if he chose to do certain things.'

'You mean you physically threatened him?'

'I suppose one could put it that way.'

'What *exactly* did you threaten to do?'

His glance was blackly amused. 'You really want to know?'

She took a deep breath. 'I really want to know.'

He leaned back on the car behind him and folded his arms. 'Just the usual. That he might wake up one night to find his kneecaps nailed to the floor and certain parts of his anatomy missing.'

'You *didn't*!' she gasped. 'You *wouldn't*!'

He laughed. 'Yes, I did, and no, I wouldn't. But he doesn't know that,' he added drily. 'Look, Salome...' He straightened, black eyes flashing. 'When your parents are Italian immigrants, and you grow up in the western suburbs of Sydney, you learn three things. One—not to react to racial abuse. Two—how to fight. And three—how to handle a bully. Your Charles is a typical bully—physically big, but with no real courage or tolerance of pain. All you have to do to get the upper hand is hurt the bastards once. After that they will heartily believe whatever physical threat you make. Of course, with a man like Charles, who does have a degree of intelligence, it doesn't hurt to have a second string to your bow, such as the threat of losing his very comfortable lifestyle. After all, I'm sure your ex-husband, if he is any sort of a man, won't appreciate his lawyer trying to assault his ex-wife. Some pressure applied from that quarter can only help. It's amazing, too, how often the pain of losing one's money can sometimes be more persuasive than the pain of losing—er—other things.'

He smiled down at her wide-eyed face, taking her elbow and leading her somewhat stunned self over to his Jaguar. What kind of man was this? she thought dazedly. So tough, so forceful, so ruthless!

'We'll go to your mother's first,' he went on in that deceptively mild tone he could adopt when he chose to play the gentleman, 'and pick up your things. I'll need to make a call from there as well. I was supposed to be at my parents' place for lunch, but there might not be time for that.'

'Your parents?' she repeated blankly.

His eyes gleamed with a sardonic light. 'Yes, I do have parents, Salome. I didn't ooze out of a man-hole up at the Cross. There's even an older brother, Angelo, as well as three younger sisters— Gina, Antonia and Therese. All respectably married. I'm the only black sheep.'

Very black, came the automatic thought.

Her mind suddenly clicked into gear. Here was her escape from going to see Ralph. 'Oh, well, then, please don't put yourself out for me. Just drop me off at Molly's and go on. You could always ring Ralph about Charles later. You shouldn't miss an important lunch-date with your parents.'

They had reached his car, and Mike inserted the key in the passenger-door. 'Hardly all that important,' he threw over his shoulder. He wrenched open the door, and stepped back to wave her inside. 'I go out to see them every Friday for lunch. They won't die of disappointment if I miss one time.'

The image of Mike as a dutiful son distracted Salome for a moment, and she just stood there. She hadn't thought of him with parents at all before now, let alone having the capacity to love and care about them, as he so obviously did. 'Where do they live?' she asked. 'Your parents...'

'Kellyville. They own a market garden.'

'Oh, but that's not far from Ralph's!' she said, before realising she was putting her foot in it.

Mike's eyebrows lifted. 'Are you suggesting we might continue on there for lunch, *together*?'

'Well, I...' Did she want that? To meet his parents? It seemed perfectly pointless and futile under the circumstances, but in an odd sort of way, yes, she did want to, did want to fill in the hazy picture of Mike's background. It seemed sad to love a man and not really know him.

'If you like,' she said lamely.

'I don't like,' he snarled.

She blinked shock at his attitude.

'You don't know my mother,' he went on testily. 'One look at you and she'll start knitting baby-bootees.'

Salome blinked again.

'My dear Salome...' he tipped up her chin with a single fingertip, looking deeply into her eyes with a dry, cynical expression '...all Italian Mammas want their sons married with a whole brood of children to spoil. You might not realise it but, dressed as you are today, you look the image of wholesome womanhood, ripe for marriage and babies!

'So much for images,' he muttered and, sliding his hand around under the weight of hair at her neck, he captured her mouth in a kiss not intended to convey anything wholesome.

Salome wished she hadn't responded, wished she had kept her lips pressed firmly together, her tongue still. But her love doomed her to failure. She moaned under his seductive onslaught, which only made matters worse. Impassioned by the sound of her arousal, his fingers tightened in the soft flesh of her neck, his mouth increasing its pressure, his free hand sliding up under her jumper to cover a single lace-cupped breast, to tease her nipple to rock-like hardness.

When he let her go she staggered back against the car. 'I think, perhaps, you'd better get in,' he ground out. 'Or shall we forget the whole damned business and go back up to bed?'

She stared at him. He meant it. He actually meant it. And, worst of all, she was tempted. God, what was she coming to, accepting this man's derision in the same breath as his kisses? Surely love didn't demand that a woman give up her self-respect, did it?

Yet if she tried to convince him he was all wrong about her he wouldn't believe her. Not that she could entirely blame him for that. She had dug her own grave with her behaviour at his restaurant over the years. Even as late as last night, she had implied that she had taken various lovers since her divorce, ones which she didn't even bother to go out with.

Then there was the way she had acted with him in bed, with such uninhibited abandon. How could she explain that away if she was to claim relative innocence? By admitting she loved him? He would laugh. Or, even worse, use her admission to corrupt her further to his wishes. For he didn't want her love, only her total submission. Which, from the way he could make her feel with a simple kiss, was not far off anyway.

Even now he was looking at her with a smug, expectant look on his face, waiting for her to agree to a return to bed.

With great difficulty Salome dredged up a semblance of a smile, letting her eyes cool as they looked up at him. They landed on his smouldering eyes, drifted down to his beckoning mouth, dropped further to his taut virility, all without so much as a visible flicker.

Once again, she was struck by her capacity to act a part. Thanks to her treacherous husband! But how well she had learnt her lessons, managing to go from tortured, aroused woman to controlled sophisticate in twenty seconds. 'They say pleasure is increased by the waiting, Mike,' she said in a voice designed to dampen even the hottest lover. 'Let's wait.'

She turned away and lowered herself gracefully into the car, sliding the seatbelt across her breasts, trying to ignore their swollen state and the way her nipples were jutting hard right through her soft bra to be outlined against the lemon wool. Her cheeks pinked under the feel of Mike's searing glare, but she refused to look up. Finally, he swung the door shut, striding around to unlock his side and climb in behind the wheel. His sidelong glance was savage as he shoved the key into the ignition, fired the engine and slammed the gear-stick into reverse. But the car remained stationary, his hand curling over the gear-stick, his knuckles whitening as he again looked daggers at her.

'That was what the fiasco in the lift was last night, wasn't it?' he pronounced harshly. 'A game of tease. You always planned to give in eventually, didn't you? Tell me, did it titillate you further, hone your undeniably voracious sexual appetite, to make me wait?'

She stared back at him and gulped. This was taking her role-playing too far. 'No,' she denied. 'It wasn't like that at all!'

He seemed taken aback by her vehemence. 'What, then?'

'I—I was embarrassed...confused... *Drunk*!' she added in desperation.

He made a scoffing sound. 'Not *that* drunk.'

She threw her head back to stare straight ahead. 'You don't have to believe me,' she said stiffly.

'I sure as hell don't! One day, Salome,' he growled, 'you'll play your sexual games with the wrong partner. In fact, I'm beginning to wonder if poor old Charles might not have been on the end of a few of them.'

Her head snapped around in automatic outrage. 'Charles needed no encouragement,' she protested. 'You don't honestly believe I'd let a man like that touch me, do you?' An involuntary shudder rippled through her, revealing the shaken, vulnerable woman she was.

Mike frowned across at her, then shook his head. 'God knows what I believe any more. You've got me stumped.'

Salome wanted to cry. She had *him* stumped? *She* was the one who was stumped! Well and truly. A crazy laugh escaped her lips before she could snatch it back.

'And what does that mean?' he flung at her.

Now she couldn't stop laughing. 'Nothing...nothing.'

He muttered something decidedly obscene, and backed out like a madman, screeching up the ramp from the basement like a teenage hoodlum showing off. But he wasn't showing off, Salome realised as her hysteria died and she saw the evidence of real pain on his face. He was hurting, hurting badly.

It shocked her. Shocked and puzzled her. Why should it bother him to believe bad things of her? He wanted her badly, didn't he? Her thoughts confused and depressed her, and she sat in silence as Mike weaved his way through the busy lanes, eating up the miles between McMahon's Point and Killara in record time.

She sagged with relief when the Jaguar screeched into the kerb outside Molly's. But, with the engine suddenly dead, the silence and tension between them was excruciating. Mike made a frustrated sound and turned towards her. 'Salome...'

Her green eyes carried true bewilderment and unhappiness as they reluctantly faced him. 'Yes?'

He sighed when he saw them. 'I'm sorry. What I said ... I didn't really mean it. I—I know you didn't lead Charles on. I know your fear and shock last night was genuine. And I know you weren't deliberately teasing me in the lift. It just happened between us, didn't it? Though why you had to run away afterwards, I'll never understand.'

Tears rushed into her eyes. Tears of relief. She hadn't realised how much his vile accusations had been tearing her apart.

'Please don't cry,' he rasped.

'No,' she agreed, blinking furiously.

'I said I was sorry. There's no reason to cry.'

No reason to cry? she thought wretchedly. No reason? Oh, Mike... if only you knew...

They both sat in silence for a minute as she got herself under control, drawing a tissue from her handbag and wiping her nose.

'Shall we go inside?' he finally suggested. 'I'll make the call to my parents while you collect your things. Maybe your mother could make us both a cup of tea?'

'I don't think she's home,' Salome said, having noticed Wayne's car was missing. 'It looks like she and Wayne have gone out. At least...' she sighed as a horn blew and a white Falcon sedan swung into the driveway in front of them '...they *were* out.'

'Hm. Wayne's not exactly popular with you, is he?' Mike commented.

Salome shrugged. 'He's all right, I guess. I hardly know him. Neither does Molly,' she added pointedly. 'Certainly not enough to have him stay.'

'He's *living* with your mother?'

'He moved in yesterday,' she said curtly.

'Ahh... I see... Hence your move to the penthouse.'

'Exactly.' Salome pushed open the car door and climbed out on to the footpath. Mike alighted from his side, a sardonic smile on his face as he walked around to join her. 'And here I was, thinking you had succumbed to the fatal attraction of living next to me.'

'Mike! Salome!' Molly called from the driveway. 'Come on in. You're just in time!'

'In time for what?' Salome muttered under her breath.

'Now, now, be nice,' Mike whispered, sliding an arm through hers. 'Besides, your mother is a grown woman, entitled to live her life as she sees fit. You demand the same rights, don't you?'

'Well, yes, but——'

'But nothing! Let the woman have her fun.'

'F-*fun*?' Salome spluttered, outraged. 'I'll have you know that she's been having fun with men since before I was born. Always at my expense, I might add. Do you have any idea what it was like, having a procession of creepy uncles living with you? Most of them young enough to be my boyfriend, instead of Molly's, with libidos to match? I had to have eyes in the back of my head, trying to outwit their octopus hands!'

Salome scooped in a deep breath, ready to launch into a further tirade when she realised that Mike was staring at her with a surprised expression on his face. Her heart lurched as it slowly changed to one of tender understanding.

'You had a rotten time growing up, didn't you?'

This unexpected sympathy flustered her. 'I...I...'

'Never mind.' His other hand came over to pat the arm he already had hold of. 'We'll talk about it later,' he soothed. 'For now I think we'd best go inside. Molly is staring over at us, frowning.'

Salome allowed her distracted self to be led like a lamb through the front gate and up the path to the porch, where her mother was indeed frowning at her.

'Whatever were you arguing about?' Molly started immediately. 'Salome, you're not being your usual stubborn self, are you? A man like Mike won't put up with your nonsense for long, you know.' She turned to Mike, all sweet smiles and feminine charm. 'She's really a very amenable girl, Mike,' she said silkily. 'But she has developed these quirks since her divorce. Firstly, she doesn't go out!

'No, Salome, don't interrupt,' she went on mercilessly when Salome made a protesting sound. 'Someone has to take you in hand. Do you realise, Mike, dear, that her date with you last night was her first outing since she left that horrid Ralph Diamond? Fancy that, a girl as lovely-looking as she is and not a single male person has she allowed inside this door in fourteen months! Yes, I can see you're shocked, and I sincerely hope you're going to remedy the situation. Don't take any nonsense from her! Just say, "Salome, we're going out and that's that!" That's the way to handle a woman, isn't it, Wayne?'

She turned to give her beaming escort a coy look, sliding an arm through his elbow and giving it a squeeze. 'That's what Wayne did to me. He said, "Molly, we're going to be married, and I'm not taking no for an answer." Not that he got one,' she smiled, waving a huge diamond engagement-ring under two startled spectators' noses. 'That's why we're celebrating. Well, you two, aren't you going to congratulate us, instead of standing there with your mouths open?'

CHAPTER TEN

SALOME'S mouth snapped shut. She wished she had been able to do the same to Molly's a minute ago. Oh, God... now Mike knew there had been no men since Ralph other than himself; he knew she had lied. She flicked a nervous glance towards his awfully still body.

Tentative green eyes met piercing black ones. Her stomach contracted.

'I'll go put the champagne on ice,' Wayne offered into the suddenly charged silence. And disappeared, obviously not comfortable with the atmosphere.

'Have I said something I oughtn't?' Molly looked genuinely perplexed. 'I thought you'd be happy to hear Wayne and I were getting married, Salome. Truly, I don't think I'll ever understand you.'

'You're not alone there,' Mike muttered low under his breath, giving Salome an exasperated glance before setting a wide smile on Molly. 'She's so delighted with your engagement, she's been struck speechless, haven't you, darling?'

Salome noticed how Molly's eyes lit up, not at Mike's reassurance, but at the word 'darling'. She could just see Molly's mind ticking over, already planning mother-daughter weddings. Yet she was too ridiculously rattled to utter a word in her own defence. It was much easier to let Mike take charge and handle the situation as he saw fit. Which he did, playing the authoritative male to the hilt, ordering her to pack while he rang his parents.

'Ohh, he's so masterful!' Molly giggled girlishly as she followed her daughter into the bedroom, and started probing for every intimate detail of the night before.

Salome was not about to give a blow-by-blow description of her long and traumatic evening, though somehow the insistent Molly managed to extract from her an admission to staying part of the night with Mike.

'I *knew* it!' Molly said smugly. 'I just knew it! What's he like in bed?'

'Mol-ly!' Salome groaned.

'All right, all right. I know you don't like talking about your sex life.'

'And please don't go making any leading comments about our getting married. Mike and I are very happy to go on just as we are.'

'What if he asks you to marry him?'

'Believe me, he won't.'

'But he loves you. Anyone can see he loves you!'

Salome laughed. 'Why? Because he calls me "darling" and wants me in his bed every night?'

'Does he?' Molly gasped. '*Every* night?'

Heat zoomed into Salome's cheeks. 'That's merely an expression. You don't have to take it literally. Come on. Be a good mother and help me pack.'

Mike contained his displeasure with Salome's having deceived him till they were back in his car and accelerating up the road that led to the highway.

'Well?' he said drily. 'Am I to get an explanation or not?'

'About what?'

'Cut the innocent act, Salome. I want the truth, and I want it *now*! Have there or have there not been any other men since your divorce?'

His aggressive tone infuriated her. 'What difference does it make?' she flung back at him. 'It won't change your opinion of me. In your eyes I'll always be a mercenary bitch who married an older man for his money and was probably having other men on the side. What does it matter if last night I let you think I'd been sleeping around since my divorce? If I'd claimed to be celibate you wouldn't have believed me!'

The truth behind her words brought a tidal wave of bitterness, and she rounded on him. 'What gives you the right to question me, anyway? You don't want a real relationship with me. Basically, you don't give a damn how many men I'd had. You're only too glad to take full advantage of my so-called experience!'

She glared her cynicism over at him. He made an exasperated sound and swung his eyes back to the road. None too soon either, as they were zooming towards a set of red lights that separated them from six lanes of busy highway traffic going the other way.

Mike slammed on his brakes and the Jaguar skidded to a halt merely inches from disaster. Salome cried out as she was thrown forward then snapped back into the front seat.

'Sorry about that,' he muttered, throwing her an apologetic look. 'Are you all right?'

She dragged in then let out a shuddering breath. 'Yes ... I suppose so.'

But she wasn't all right. She knew she couldn't go on like this, trapped by love in a situation in which she couldn't win, no matter what she did.

'You're wrong, you know,' he surprised her by saying once they had joined the main stream of traffic that led away from the city. 'I do want a real relationship with you. I asked you to live with me, didn't I? *You're* the one who doesn't want it. *You're* the one who's trying to keep our involvement on a casual basis. Not only do you tell me nothing about yourself, you deliberately mislead me. OK, I agree I would have had a hard time believing you hadn't slept with a man since your divorce. But I concede it's possible.'

All she could do was stare across at him. This was Michael Angellini talking? The man whom she'd always thought would never concede an inch where her morals were concerned?

'Hell, I can even understand why you married a man like Diamond,' he went on brusquely. 'With your background and looks, you couldn't have helped being set on a sexual path early in life. When Diamond came along with his wealth and position and privilege, he must have been an enormous temptation to try your wiles on.'

Salome's heart sank again. This was familiar territory. Mike hadn't changed his mind about her being a promiscuous, gold-digging little tramp. The only difference was he now understood *why* it was so.

'Anyway, that's past history,' he said determinedly. 'Irrelevant. It's the woman you are now that I'm interested in, the woman I spent the night with. I want to be with that woman, Salome. And not just occasionally. Move in with me, live with me.'

She looked at the smouldering desire in his eyes and slowly shook her head. She had been down that path before, and she didn't like it.

'Goddam it, Salome, I can't work you out! One moment you accuse me of not wanting a real relationship with you, then, when I offer you one, you throw it back in my face. For pity's sake, what *do* you want from me?'

Her gaze fastened on his almost pouting and very beautiful mouth, the stubborn set of his jaw, her heart turning over as wave upon wave of emotion lapped through her. I want you to love me, came the silent, heart-wrenching answer. She sighed. 'Your respect would be a nice place to start,' she said drily.

His eyes stabbed pure disbelief at her before returning to the road. 'What is this?' he growled. 'Regret about last night? Good grief, Salome, I think this world has moved on from the old double standards, as well as the hackneyed "he won't respect me in the morning" bit!'

'*Has* it?' she questioned cynically. 'You forget, Mike, I've seen the results of a woman being easy in matters of sex. And the old double standards still apply. Scoff if you like, but I don't believe in moving in with a man unless one knows him very, very well. OK, so Molly was lucky this time with Wayne. He seems to really care about her.

But there have been plenty of men she's lived with who didn't, men who betrayed what they thought of her before they left, with their fists as well as their words.'

Mike's glance was appalled. 'My God . . . !'

There was a short, sharp silence as Mike drove on, his brow furrowed with deep thought. Suddenly his head whipped sidewards, black eyes even more horrified. 'You're not saying that's what you think I am, are you? A man who would beat a woman?'

Her sigh was deep. 'Of course not. All I'm saying is I refuse to be rushed into anything when we hardly know each other.'

'Hardly know each other?' he spluttered. 'I've known you for damned well years!'

'Not the real me, you haven't,' she bit out.

'The real you? What the hell does that mean?'

'It means exactly that!' she retorted. 'The real me. Salome Twynan. Not Mrs Ralph Diamond. Not the public image. Not . . . what I used to project at your restaurant.'

'Care to elaborate on that last part?' he ground out.

Salome wished she hadn't started on this, but she was trapped now and had no option but to go on. 'I . . . I know what you thought of me, and I used to play the seductive siren out of . . . spite.'

'Spite?'

'Yes. You made me so mad, judging me without really knowing me.'

'*I* made *you* mad?' Mike exclaimed.

Salome swallowed, remembering all too clearly what he had admitted to thinking about her, what he had wanted to do.

Hornsby came and went, with Mike having fallen peevishly silent after she'd declined to continue her own defence. When Salome saw the sign that indicated the turn-off to Dural, her stomach tightened. She had almost forgotten where they were going, forgotten about Ralph and Charles. She stared agitatedly through the passenger window, watching with a growing apprehension as the suburban Sydney gradually gave way to gently undulating countryside.

'You'll have to direct me to Ralph's place,' Mike said abruptly as they approached Dural.

Her eyes returned to the front. 'Just keep going on this road till I tell you. It's a while yet.'

'How did you meet a man like Ralph Diamond?' Mike asked after a few seconds' awkward silence. 'I mean, were you his secretary or something?'

Salome almost laughed. 'No; I was a waitress at the time.' This brought a startled glance. 'Believe me, Mike,' she said drily, 'I didn't always look or act or talk the way I do now. I actually left school at fifteen—not because I was all that dumb, but because I'd had so many changes of school, with Molly living here and there and everywhere, that I kept falling behind. And then there was the problem of making ends meet. My mother was not always the best at that. A working daughter was preferable to a fully dependent student.'

'I can imagine,' Mike nodded ruefully. 'So you were working as a waitress. How did you meet a multi-millionaire? Did you wait tables for him at one of the top restaurants?'

'No, I used to do extra work at weekends for a catering firm that specialised in home-based celebrations. They were hired for Ralph's forty-ninth birthday party, and instructed to send along the best-looking female waitresses they could find. I was one of them. And, before you jump to conclusions, we were for decorative purposes only. Nothing else.'

'And Ralph liked your particular brand of decoration?'

'It seems so. Not that he made a line for me during the party. The night was actually drawing to an end when one of his drunken guests started sexually harassing me. I pushed the pain in the neck in the swimming-pool. The man got angry and dragged me in too, where he tried to rip my clothes off in the water. I almost drowned in the ensuing fight. Ralph rescued me, threw the man out, gave my rather hysterical self a sedative, and put me to bed in one of the guest rooms.'

'Convenient.' There was a sardonic edge to Mike's voice. Salome decided he would think what he wanted to think no matter what she said, so she just continued with the facts.

'He woke me up the next morning, gave me breakfast, then drove me home. At the door he shocked the life out of me by asking me out. I thought he was way too old for me, but I was flattered and went. Three months later we were married.'

'A regular whirlwind courtship.'

She sighed at his scoffing tone. 'He said he loved me, Mike, and I believed him. One isn't always a good judge of such things at eighteen,' she added wearily. His head whipped around, the car hitting the gravel as it swerved dangerously. 'Hey, watch it!' she shouted.

He swung the wheel back round, swearing volubly.

'What on earth's the matter with you?' she gasped. 'That's the second time you've nearly killed us today!'

He muttered something under his breath, then startled her by pulling over to the side of the road and cutting the engine. He took a deep breath then twisted round to face her, his eyes darkly troubled. 'You were only *eighteen* when you married Ralph?'

'No,' she said, frowning herself. 'I was eighteen when we met. I turned nineteen the week before we were married.'

Mike looked as if he couldn't believe what he was hearing. 'How old were you when *we* met, when you first came to Angellini's?'

She was flustered by his demandingly urgent voice, his undoubted shock. 'Still nineteen. Almost twenty.'

His frown darkened. 'And now? How old are you *now*?'

'Twenty-four.'

'Twenty-four...'

'Mike, I've never deliberately hidden my age. How old did you think I was?' she asked.

'Older,' he said, obviously shaken. 'Much older.'

Salome shook her head in confusion. 'How much older?'

He shrugged. 'About thirty, I guess. Not that you look *old*. But you seemed around twenty-five when we first met. God, no wonder Molly looks so young. She *is* young!' He went to say something further, but changed his mind, shaking his head and grumbling under his breath.

Salome could not fathom why he was so upset about her age, unless he felt that, at eighteen, she was unlikely to be the callous sexual manipulator he had always believed her to be. Perhaps he felt guilty about his opinion of her all these years. Perhaps he was beginning to wonder if he'd made a mistake in his assessment of her character.

Her heart leapt with hope, her eyes flying to his frowning face. 'Mike...?'

He lifted still troubled eyes. 'Yes?'

She wanted to say that she was not promiscuous and never had been. She wanted to explain about Ralph's supposed impotency. Above all, she wanted to tell Mike *he* was the first man she had ever really loved. But somehow the confessions stuck in her throat. She couldn't bear to see his disbelief, hear his laughter or his scorn.

'Yes?' he repeated impatiently.

'What does it matter how old I am?' she blurted out. 'What difference does it make?'

He glared at her for a moment, then looked away. 'No damned difference now, I suppose. What's done is done, but by God I'm going to give Ralph Diamond a piece of my mind—the bastard!' His eyes were back to hard black. 'Which way do we go from here?' he gruffed as he fired the engine and accelerated off. 'We must be getting close.'

Salome put her mind on her immediate surroundings with great difficulty. Angry and simmering with suppressed violence, Mike was an alarming person. 'Take...take the second turning on the right,' she said shakily. 'Ralph's place is a Spanish-style house behind a high white fence about a mile down on the right.'

'You'd better get down,' he grumped after he had followed her directions.

A desperate plea for him please to forget Ralph, to turn round, to go back, rose in her throat. But one look at his grimly determined face told her such an action was hopeless. Numb fingers undid her seatbelt, and she slid down the seat, feeling sick.

In no time the car turned sharply into a driveway and crunched to a halt. Mike operated the button that rolled down his window, and cool winter air blew in, though Salome doubted her shiver was from the cold.

She huddled there, silent and strained, listening to the whirring sound of the cameras on the gateposts, which turned to survey who it was who dared to intrude on Ralph Diamond's privacy. She shook her head. She knew the sound only too well, knew what she would hear next.

A crisp male voice—not Ralph's—spoke from a speaker built into the post. 'Who is it, and what do you want?' it demanded abruptly.

'Mike Angellini to see Mr Diamond.'

'Mr Diamond is not in residence at the moment.'

'Then where would I find him?'

'Sorry. I'm not at liberty to give out that information.'

'See?' Salome hissed.

'Can I speak to his secretary, please?' Mike persisted in an authoritative tone.

'Miss Bath is also unavailable. And I'm not at liberty——'

'Look, mate,' Mike rapped out. 'I'm not interested in what you're not at liberty to. I *am* interested in common decency, so I strongly suggest you get yourself down to this gate personally, or there won't be a gate any more. It's surprising what a Jaguar can do at full speed.'

Salome gulped. She should have known Mike wouldn't go away meekly. 'I'll be with you shortly, Mr Angellini,' came the grudging concession.

'You might as well get up now,' Mike directed towards Salome as he began to climb out. 'The cameras have stopped.'

Salome levered herself up into the seat, half relieved, half petrified. She was just in time to see a very large security guard striding down the gravel driveway, a menacing Dobermann by his side.

The ensuing discussion between Mike and the guard was heated to say the least, Mike demanding to know where either Mr Diamond or Miss Bath could be contacted. The guard insisted he didn't know, but in the end admitted that Miss Bath would probably be returning to the property later that evening, and would be informed that there was an emergency concerning Mr Diamond's ex-wife. Mike was still furious when he climbed back into the car, thumping the steering-wheel angrily.

'You did your best,' she soothed.

His eyes glittered dangerously as they lanced towards her. 'Don't try to make me feel better, Salome,' he grated out. 'I'm an arrogant fool who always thinks he has all the answers. Now it seems I haven't.'

She was startled by this unexpected outburst.

'I thought I had *you* taped,' he went on agitatedly. 'I thought I knew what made you tick. Now nothing's fitting the pre-programmed picture any more!'

She didn't know what to say.

He shook his head in frustration. 'Not only do I find out you haven't been bed-hopping since your divorce, but also that you were little more than a *child* when you married Diamond. Hell, I know what a girl is like at eighteen! I have three sisters. I know how vulnerable they were at that age, how often they imagined themselves in love, how easily it would have been for an older, more experienced man to con them, to get them into bed. Ralph Diamond should have been hung, drawn and quartered for what he did to you. No matter how experienced or grown up you might have thought you were at that age, you were still a babe in arms compared to him. To take a young girl, to marry her and corrupt her into what he wanted for his own gratification, without caring, without love, is——'

'But it wasn't like that!' she broke in. 'I know now Ralph wasn't as perfect as I'd once thought, but he...he was good to me. I—I really believed he loved me, and I was positive I loved him! The reason there's been no men since is because I've been so horribly shattered by the way he threw me out. It...it was only when you came along recently that I realised——' Her voice cut off. To say she realised that she didn't love Ralph after all was too much of an admission.

'That you realised what?' Mike probed, setting penetrating black eyes upon her.

She swallowed the lump in her throat. 'That I was finally over Ralph and that I...I wanted to have an affair.'

He stared at her for an agonisingly long time. 'Tell me,' he said at last, his tone low, almost wary. 'Is it just sex, or do you care for me at all?'

Panic set in. To tell him she loved him would be the ultimate naïveté. 'I—I find you extremely attractive,' she conceded.

'Oh, terrific! Very flattering.' His laugh was self-derisive as he fired the engine, sending the gravel spraying as he reversed out of the driveway. 'Hell, I doubt my ego is going to survive having an affair with you, Salome,' he threw at her. 'I doubt *I'm* going to survive it, if the last twenty-four hours are anything to go by. No, don't say a word! I asked for it and I got it. Let's leave it at that.'

He slammed his foot down and the car screeched away, leaving Salome in a whirl, both from his driving and the questions his attitude had left spinning round in her mind. *Could* he be falling in love with her? Was that why he wanted to know if she truly cared for him? It didn't seem possible. And yet...

CHAPTER ELEVEN

THE Angellini farm at Kellyville was a small
concern, most of its ten acres under cultivation,
with a fairly new two-storeyed brick home sitting
to one side of a ramshackle shed-like structure.
As Mike directed the Jaguar slowly along the dirt
driveway and around the recent rain-made pot-
holes, Salome wondered if the shed had once been
the Angellini home. If so, there had been a time
when Mike had been very, very poor. Her heart
went out to him. She knew what that was like.

'There's Dad over there with his prized Brussels
sprouts,' he pointed out, winding down the
window, waving and shouting. There were waves
and shouts in return.

'You call him Dad?' she remarked. 'That's not
very Italian.'

He shrugged. 'I was born in Australia, Salome,
brought up as an Australian. Most Australians
call their father "Dad".'

Salome looked at his stubbornly set mouth,
and wondered just how much racial prejudice
he'd had to suffer during his growing-up years.
Too much, she decided, though the 'I'll show
them' attitude would probably have fired an extra
surge of ambition in his very proud breast. 'How
did you get to be a restaurateur?' she asked as
they approached the house.

He cast her an exasperated glance. 'Question time, Salome? *Now?*'

'Why not now?'

'Because any second my mother is going to descend on us, and then you'll know why not now. But, in a nutshell, it all started while I was working my way through a business degree by working nights as a barman in a restaurant. One night the *maître d'* collapsed, ill. I took over. For some weird and wonderful reason I was a huge success. The clientele doubled in no time.'

All women, no doubt, Salome thought caustically. And wasn't it just like him to be smart as well? A business degree, no less. The man was a menace!

'The owner made a fortune,' he went on, swinging the car to a halt beside the neatly bedded flower-gardens that flanked the front steps of the house. 'So when I graduated I worked for a while as a financial investor in a bank, saved my money, then, with an appropriate loan, went into the restaurant business. Hence, Angellini's. Actually, there's an Angellini's in every capital city of Australia. Next year I'll be opening several more.'

'I didn't know that,' she said, though not surprised. She recognised a dynamo when she saw one.

The sight of a large handsome woman in a black dress bearing down upon them brought a low groan from Mike. 'For God's sake, don't say much. And don't admit to anything.'

Totally unnecessary advice, Salome was to think within seconds of meeting his mother,

Claudia. She didn't let too many people get a word in edgeways.

'Michael, you're late!' she pronounced in a thick Italian accent, with a savage waving of her finger. When he climbed out and went to say something he was subjected to a fierce bear-hug and many kisses. Salome had difficulty suppressing her smiles as she saw Mike go red with embarrassment. Quite a feat, considering his olive skin.

'And what are these clothes you are wearing?' Claudia admonished her son further. 'You look like one of those bikies. Next thing you'll be driving up on a motorcycle! Really, Michael, I do not approve; I——' She broke off, directing a surprised but not unhappy glance as Salome emerged from her side of the Jaguar. 'Michael, you naughty boy, you bring a girlfriend home and you give me no warning? Why didn't you tell me when you called, eh? I could have at least prepared something special!'

'Mum,' he said at last, 'my usual Friday lunch is a feast compared to what some people eat. Salome wouldn't mind if it was just sandwiches, would you, darling?' He put out his hand, and she walked around and took it.

The word 'darling' did as much for Mrs Angellini as it had for Molly. 'Salome,' she gushed, beaming. 'What a lovely name!' Then she frowned. 'It does not go so well with Angellini, though, does it, eh?'

Mike slipped Salome a sardonic glance. See, it said, wedding bells already!

'Are you hounding the boy about getting married again, woman?' a deeply accented voice resounded behind Salome. She turned to see Mike's father walking towards them, smiling and wiping large hands on a checked handkerchief.

Salome could see now where Mike got his looks. Nearing sixty, Giuseppe Angellini was still a striking man. His black, wavy hair, though streaked liberally with grey, was thick and lustrous, his broad-shouldered body very fit-looking. Wicked black eyes danced knowingly as they roved over Salome's body, and she almost gasped. Why, the old devil! she thought laughingly.

'Though this time I agree with Mamma,' he smiled. 'A woman such as this should not be allowed to get away. What are you waiting for, my son? Some other man to snatch her from under your nose? If I myself were not married . . .'

'Giuseppe,' Claudia warned, a definite flash of jealousy in her big brown eyes. 'Stop flirting. Holy Mother of God, I have to watch this man every minute! Come,' she threw at all of them. 'It's too cold standing out here. We should be inside in front of the fire, having a nice drink of *vino*, and catching up on your news, Michael. There is so much I wish to ask.' She came forward and took Salome's arm. 'The naughty boy tells me nothing, you know. Would you not think he would want to tell his mamma all his comings and goings?'

As she was led away, solidly captive in Claudia's arm, Salome threw a desperate glance back over her shoulder at Mike. He was busy talking to his father, but lifted an eyebrow at her, as if to say, 'This was your idea, remember?'

And she was not really regretting it, although slightly worried at what questions she might have to fend off. There was a quiet joy in seeing a side to Mike that wasn't hard or cold or dangerously overwhelming. As a son he was very human, a warmer and more vulnerable person, a person capable of loving, a person worth loving.

The thought surfaced again that he might care about her more than she had first thought, more than maybe he even knew himself. Salome was very familiar with self-deception when it came to matters of the heart. But she wasn't going to bargain on it. A man's love was a rare thing, she believed. They were more comfortable with lust.

'I am very happy to see Michael with such a *nice* girl,' his mother was saying as she deposited Salome in front of the open fire in the living-room. 'Not one of those glamour-pusses I've seen him photographed with in the magazines.'

Salome felt colour creep up her neck. Next thing she was going to ask about her background. 'I...I like your home,' she complimented by way of distraction.

'Michael bought it for us,' Claudia said proudly. 'He's bought things for all the family. He's been a big success in life, has my Michael. All he needs now is a wife and a family of his own.'

Salome tensed, then sighed with relief when Mike appeared.

'Dad's gone off to shower and change,' he said.

'You get Salome a glass of wine, then, Michael,' his mother decided, 'while I lay out the food.'

'Thank God you came!' Salome whispered as Claudia disappeared. 'Things were getting sticky.'

'I could always say we have to leave soon,' he offered.

'Oh, no, we couldn't do that. It would hurt them, and they're really very sweet, Mike. All they want is for you to be happy.'

His eyes met hers and held them for a long moment, his expression admiring, but puzzled. 'You are an enigma,' he murmured, sliding both arms around her waist and drawing her to him. 'Which is the real you, Salome? Fire or ice? Hard or soft? Indifferent or caring?'

He bent to take her mouth in a brief, hungry kiss. 'God, you're like a disease!' he rasped. 'A damned infernal disease for which there's no known cure.' Groaning, he kissed her again, was still kissing her when his mother walked back in.

Rather than being embarrassed, Claudia seemed pleased. In fact, she didn't stop smiling smugly at both of them for the rest of their visit. Salome, for her part, felt a little guilty that Mike's parents thought a wedding was afoot. It seemed a shame to give them false hopes. And they *were* false. Even if Mike did love her, he would never marry her.

'They think we're going to get married,' she said unhappily as they drove off.

'Well, I did warn you,' he countered sharply. 'It seems to be an Italian failing, wanting their children married and having a horde of *bam-*

binos. I'm the only one of their children who isn't doing so, and they think it reflects on them somehow. I've long ceased to worry about it. Now shut up, Salome. I'm running late, and will have to concentrate on the road if I'm to get to work on time.'

They arrived back at McMahon's Point at twenty-past five after a hair-raising drive. Despite running very late, Mike still collected her new keys for her from the janitor, then stopped to give her a lingering kiss at her penthouse door. 'Are you sure you won't move in with me?' he tried again when they were both breathing hard.

'No,' she resisted staunchly, though her body was screaming 'yes'.

He grimaced. 'You're not just teasing me?'

'No.'

He hesitated, raking her face with a penetrating gaze. 'I wish I knew what you were thinking. I wish...' He sighed. 'You'll wait up for me?'

'Yes.'

'Can't you say anything else other than "yes" and "no"?' he demanded irritably.

She smiled. 'What would you like me to say?'

His eyes flashed, his hands turning fierce on her, digging into her arms. 'Tell me you can't bear to be away from me,' he ground out. 'Tell me the hours will drag till I'm with you. Tell me you love me, dammit!'

Her whole insides somersaulted, her mind stunned by what his passionate demand had betrayed. He loved her. He must! She lifted a shaking hand to trace over his angry mouth, her eyes misting. 'I can't bear to be away from you,' she whispered. 'The hours will drag till you're with me ... I love you, Michael Angellini.'

His hands froze on her arms, then slipped away, dropping to his side. He took a step back and just stared at her. There was a hell in his eyes, a hell of uncertainty and suspicion. 'Don't play games with me, Salome.'

'I'm not,' she denied, shaken by the torment in his face.

He swept her back into his arms. 'Say it again,' he rasped.

'I love you.'

'And again! No, no more, I can't stand it!' he groaned. 'I have to go to work, and if you say it again I won't be responsible. God, do you know how I've longed for those words?' He cupped her cheeks and drenched her upturned face with kisses. 'I've loved you for so long, right from the first moment I saw you. You've been my agony and ecstasy, my heaven and hell. Say you'll move in with me when I come home tonight. Send me away with your "yes" ringing in my ears.'

'Yes,' she said. 'Oh, yes!'

Salome spent the next hour in a daze. He loved her. He'd always loved her. She walked aimlessly about, little thrills of joy rippling through her. *Always*. She could think of nothing else.

The jangling of the telephone snapped her out of it, the seemingly urgent sound bringing a sudden tightening to her nerves. Who could it be? Molly? She hurried to the living area, and snatched up the receiver. 'Yes?'

'Miss Twynan?'

'Yes...'

'This is security downstairs. We have a Miss Valerie Bath here wishing to see you. Is it OK if we let her come up?'

Valerie? Salome was astounded, till she realised Ralph's secretary must have been given the message Mike had left at Dural. But to come here personally—it wasn't like her. She could easily have rung.

'Miss Twynan?'

'Yes... yes, she can come up,' she answered, suddenly agitated. She started pacing up and down as she awaited the secretary's arrival, unconsciously wringing her hands.

Valerie had invariably made Salome feel on edge when she was around. In her early forties, she was, to all intents and purposes, the perfect spinster secretary, being smartly groomed and attractive without being too beautiful, and efficient without being officious. She had never said an unkind or bitchy word to Salome, yet she had still managed to convey the oddest impression of pity for Salome as Ralph's wife.

Though, to be fair, Valerie alone had been kind to her the day Ralph had thrown her out, showing visibly how upset she was at her boss's cruel behaviour. Once she had even called Ralph a bastard to his face. Yet she hadn't been fired, Salome realised, frowning.

Salome answered the knock on the door with some trepidation, but was not remotely prepared for what she was to see.

'Valerie!' she gasped, shocked to find the other woman in a dreadful state. Her usually impeccable clothes were awry, her normally neat ash-brown curls in disarray. And there were tears streaming down her ravaged face. Totally thrown, Salome drew the desolate secretary into the penthouse, shutting the door behind them. With an arm around her shoulders, she edged the weeping and forlorn figure over to one of the leather sofas, settling her in a corner before dashing to the bar and pouring a large brandy.

'Here...' She pressed the glass into shaking hands and helped it up to the woman's mouth. Valerie sipped, then sobbed, then sipped again.

'I—I'm sorry,' she said at last when she had partial control of herself. 'I thought I was all right, then...' Another sob shook her.

A peculiar premonition washed through Salome and the blood drained from her face. She dropped down beside the secretary. 'It's Ralph, isn't it?' she choked out. 'He's dead. He's been killed.'

Shocked eyes stared at her. 'No. Yes. No... He...he wasn't killed, Salome. He died. This morning. He had a heart attack, but he was already in the hospital, being treated for terminal cancer.'

For a second Salome just sat there, stunned. Ralph...dead. Ralph...already dying. Cancer... All emotion seemed suspended in her. Nothing seemed real any more.

'How...how long had he had cancer?' she asked like a robot.

Valerie looked uncomfortable. 'He found out the day he—he——'

She broke off when she saw realisation dawn on Salome's face. 'The day he got rid of me,' Salome finished, shaking her head in disbelief and desolation. 'Oh, dear heaven . . . there wasn't any other woman, was there?'

Valerie looked taken aback. 'Other woman? What made you think there was another woman? There couldn't have been. Ralph's been impotent for several years.'

For a second Salome was also taken aback. She had no idea Ralph's secretary had known his secret. He'd been adamant that no one find out, always insisting on their being very affectionate to each other in public. But then, she supposed Valerie might have had access to his medical records . . .

'Salome? What made you think there was another woman?'

'He was seen with a woman. Here. A young brunette.'

'Oh, *her*. She was his private nurse. Ralph bought this place to stay in after his radiation treatments. He used to be too weak and sick sometimes to travel back to Dural.'

'But I was told he looked well!' Salome protested, as though she could argue away the feelings that were besieging her. The guilt . . . the dismay . . .

The other woman sighed wearily. 'He never wanted people to know. He used to put on an act, and in actual fact he didn't look too bad till recently. The wig helped.'

Salome flinched. Of course! It was a wig...
He had lost his hair through the chemotherapy.
Oh, God...

A black grief swept in, and she knew then that,
even if she hadn't loved Ralph as a woman should
love her husband, even if it had only been that
which a pupil gave a teacher, a ward gave her
guardian, it had been love all the same. It was
only natural and right that she should have been
at his side in death.

'You should have told me, Valerie. No matter
what Ralph said, you should have told me.'
Emotion propelled her to her feet, her voice
shaking. 'I was his wife. Can't you see how much
he loved me? So much that he was being cruel
to be kind. He didn't want me to see him waste
away, die a horrible death.' A sob caught in her
throat. 'Poor, dear, generous Ralph!'

The crumpled figure on the sofa looked up,
her face haggard and unhappy as she faced
Salome. 'I can't let you deceive yourself, my
dear,' she said in a sad voice. 'Oh, Ralph did
love you, in his own selfishly arrogant way. Or
at least he loved seeing himself through your
grateful and adoring eyes. But he didn't send you
away and divorce you for *your* sake. The fact is,
from the moment the doctors told him the truth,
he couldn't bear to have you around him any
more. His lovely young wife, so full of life and
vitality, when he was ill. Most of all, his vanity
couldn't bear to have you see that he was human,
and not some god.'

Valerie heaved in a deep, shuddering sigh
before going on. 'If you think I don't know what

I'm talking about, then I assure you you're mistaken. I came to work for Ralph Diamond nearly twenty years ago, and I knew him better than anyone, knew what he was capable of. And the one thing he wasn't capable of was understanding the feelings of others. Sit down. Let me tell you a little story...'

The unhappy woman scooped in another deep breath, and Salome sank back down on the sofa.

'When I started to work for Ralph I was still a virgin, waiting idealistically for the right man to come along. Within a few days I was neither, having been seduced and enslaved by a man who thrived on the powerful feeling of having women in love with him. That was one of the reasons he never married before—because he liked variety, liked the challenge of new relationships. I was just another feather in his cap. Within another couple of months he ended our private relationship, but he had no qualms keeping me on, basking in my now unrequited love, knowing how I felt, but basically uncaring, indifferent. It suited his purpose to have a devoted, loyal secretary—one who would do anything for him in the hope that one day he——'

Her voice faltered for a moment. 'I always thought,' she went on ruefully, 'that his impotency was a punishment from God. You could have knocked me over with a feather when he became engaged to a young thing like you, though I could see you were too smitten by Ralph playing his charming Godfather role to see straight. I wanted to warn you about Ralph's dark side, but I dared not say anything to his special protégée. He would have cut me out of his life altogether if I had. He told me one night that he was going to transform you into what he called the "perfect rich man's wife". In a warped sort of way he imagined he had done you a favour, by casting you off so that you could ensnare what he called a "more suitable fish". I presume he meant an equally wealthy but virile man, one who could give you the children he couldn't.'

Salome could do nothing but shake her head.

Ralph's secretary leaned over and took her cold hands within hers. 'Don't feel too badly, my dear. He held more affection for you than any of his other women. And I think that finally his conscience must have been getting the better of him. Only a couple of weeks ago he decided he wanted to know what you were doing with your life. He claimed it was only curiosity, but I don't think so. I think it was a type of guilt. He hired a private detective, and when he found out you were working in a dress shop and living a very quiet life with your mother he was most disturbed, said you were wasted without the proper man in your life.'

Valerie gave a wry smile. 'Typical of Ralph and his ego; he got this ridiculous idea that he could direct your life from afar, make you do what he wanted you to do without your guessing. So he gave you this penthouse, muttering away to himself that he knew something you didn't know, that if he threw certain chemicals together a certain reaction was inevitable. God knows what he had in mind. Matching you up with some man who lived in this building, I suppose.'

All the blood drained from Salome's face.

'Don't look so devastated, my dear,' Valerie soothed. 'He really wasn't himself, you know, and there's no harm done, is there? At least you got this lovely penthouse. Oh, and you did get your car, didn't you? When Ralph told me he was giving you this place, I reminded him about the car, which had been sitting idle out in the garages ever since you left. I don't think he'd even noticed.'

'Yes, I got the car,' Salome said numbly, her mind reeling. Surely Mike hadn't been in on all this, had he? Somehow she couldn't get out of her mind his frowning when he'd thought she wasn't going to move into the penthouse. Had that been because she wasn't doing things according to his and Ralph's plan? Was Mike's coming over and knocking on the door just a ruse to see her? Was his pretence that he hadn't known Ralph had given her this place a clever lie?

But... but he had said he loved her. Surely...

A lot of men say that, she reminded herself, to get a woman into their bed. *And* to keep her there.

Valerie drew her hands away, and stood up. 'I really must be going, Salome. I have a lot to do and organise. There's no one else. Believe it or not, last night Charles Smeaton was arrested on a drunken driving and negligence charge. Incredible, isn't it? Just when I need him to make all the legal arrangements.' She sighed, and her face took on a far-away look. 'Funny... I keep telling myself that Ralph has done the women in his life a favour by dying, that we can get on with our own lives. But...' She shook her head and smiled sadly, giving Salome a resigned look. 'I'll ring you, my dear, and let you know the funeral arrangements. You'll want to come, won't you?'

Salome stood up on leaden legs. 'Yes,' she said shakily. 'I'll want to come, but...you won't be able to reach me here,' she told her, firming her voice. 'Ring me at my mother's home. At Killara.'

CHAPTER TWELVE

WHEN Mike knocked on her door shortly after one, Salome felt hopelessly agitated. But she knew what she had to do.

Naturally she had forgotten the physical effect he had on her. He gave her a brief but arousing kiss as he swept in, dashingly handsome in his black dinner-suit. 'All packed, I see,' he said, smiling at the luggage.

'Yes,' she bit out, stomach churning.

Suddenly he sensed something was wrong, and a swift frown darkened his face. 'What's happened?' he asked sharply.

Salome turned away from him and walked over to one of the sofas, and sat down. If she hadn't she might have fallen down. 'Ralph's dead,' she blurted out. 'This morning. Heart attack.'

'Good lord!'

'He was already dying of cancer,' Salome went on, all the while trying to watch for a sign of guilt. 'His secretary was here tonight and told me. She told me a lot of other things too, like how Ralph ended our marriage merely because he didn't want someone young and healthy around while he was dying. So you were right. There *was* no other woman. But I was right too. He didn't love me. Valerie also confessed that *she* loved Ralph, and had been his mistress years ago.'

'Salome...darling,' Mike began sympatheti-
cally, sitting down beside her.

'Please let me finish,' she said curtly before he
could do anything like take her in his arms.
'Valerie also told me about a masterful plan
Ralph thought up just recently where I was concerned. He didn't like it, you see, that all his good
work of transforming me into the perfect partner
for a man—amend that to a *rich* man—was going
to waste. You know the sort of partner I mean.
Suitably decorative but weak and willing to
please. So he gave me this penthouse with the
underlying idea that by doing so he was giving
me to *you*.'

She saw his eyes widen, his head jerk back.
'What?'

Salome's battered soul resisted believing his
outer display of innocence. 'You heard me, Mike.
And I think you knew all about it. Don't take
me for a gullible fool. I've learnt some hard
lessons over the past fourteen months, most of
them tonight, and I don't intend to forget them.'

His black gaze was penetrating and thoughtful.
'Now let me get this straight,' he rapped out.
'You think that somehow I had a plan going with
Ralph to secure you as my mistress or lover or
what have you, is that it?'

'Got it in one.' Her tone was bitter and cynical,
but her heart was breaking. There was no love
left in Mike's face now. Only black anger. 'Valerie
said that was why Ralph gave me this penthouse,
to bring me into easy physical contact with some
rich man in this building. You are the only man
who makes sense. Not only that, I remember very

clearly how you reacted when I said I *wasn't* moving in. You were most put out. Tell me how it was, Mike, did you both sit around and talk about me? Did you both magnanimously decide not to waste Ralph's special little protégée?'

'Special little protégée?' Mike repeated in a puzzled tone.

'That's how Ralph thought of me,' she said with a bitter laugh. 'Didn't you know? I'm sure you did. He must have told you. He told his secretary. He... he moulded me, you see, into what he wanted. And I let him. I let him because... it was easier... much easier than always being the strong one, having to pick up Molly's pieces after each disastrous affair, trying to look after her, making sure the rent was paid, or the electricity bill. I... I really thought I loved him. I can see now he was just the father I never had... and always wanted...'

Salome began to crumple then, her knees buckling, tears spilling over down her cheeks.

Mike didn't let her collapse. He was up on his feet and scooping her up into his arms, sinking back down on the sofa, taking her with him and cradling her in his lap. He held her tight and rocked her till the sobs subsided, then he looked down into her tear-washed eyes with both reproach and understanding.

'I love you, Salome,' he stated unequivocally. 'I've always loved you. I did *not* talk to Ralph about you. But, yes, I *was* put out when I thought you weren't moving in here. I wanted you near me. I wanted to see you, even if only occasionally. Pass you in the hall, stand with you in the lift, smell your perfume... Anything!'

His right hand lifted to push some curls back from her face, to stroke her brow and temple in a soft, soothing rhythm. 'I love you,' he repeated. 'I planned nothing, plotted nothing. All I am guilty of is not coming after you myself when I knew you were free. I was tempted to, believe me. But I was afraid.'

Her heart leapt at Mike admitting such a thing. 'Afraid?'

'Yes... I'd been hurt once before, when I was young and poor, by a girl who claimed to love me then tossed me over for a richer older man. It embittered me for a long time, so that when I met you, while I fell in love with you at first sight, I also transferred all my old hates on to you, convinced you couldn't be anything other than a heartless, ambitious, calculating bitch. When I heard you and Diamond were divorced, I was torn. I wanted to go after you, yet I couldn't bring myself to take the first step. Nevertheless, when you turned up on my doorstep, I couldn't resist trying anything to be with you.'

He bent and kissed her, sweetly, adoringly. 'I know now you're not at all like I thought you were,' he murmured. 'You're good and kind and enchanting, but with a wild, wonderful, passionate side that takes my breath away. I know now you must have thought you loved Diamond, but I always knew you didn't, Salome. You couldn't have loved him and looked at me the way you did. That was one of the things that tormented me. I sensed that it was *me* you wanted, if only sexually, not him.'

'Yes,' she whispered. 'Yes...'

His face twisted with remembered pain. 'Did you know it back then, Salome? Did you?'

She shook her head from side to side. 'No. I think I was too young and naïve to recognise that a seemingly happily married woman could fall in love elsewhere. I did love Ralph. But not as a wife should love her husband. Still, at the time, my belief in this love left me no option but to turn the chemistry between us into anger and spite against you. When I think of how I must have confused and hurt you with my silly behaviour, I feel torn with guilt.'

He groaned. 'No more guilty than I. I was a pig to you. But it was my only release from the agony I used to feel every time you left to go home with Diamond. I kept picturing you in bed together later, with him giving you the pleasure I should have been giving you. I tried to forget you with other women, but it was hopeless. I kept picking up women who had red-gold hair or green eyes. But afterwards I would see that it wasn't you, and I'd feel sick. Sick...'

Salome lifted her hands to cradle his face, her heart racing with nerves as she realised the moment had come to tell him the whole truth. 'Mike...I never slept with Ralph. He—he couldn't make love. He told me so before we married...'

Mike's beautiful black eyes were filled with an awestruck surprise. 'But—but why did you marry him, Salome—a passionate woman like yourself?'

Her answering smile was slightly shy. 'I'm only passionate with you, Mike. By the time I met Ralph I'd already lost my virginity in a teenage love-affair, and, quite frankly, I hadn't enjoyed sex at all. At the time, in an odd kind of way, I was relieved. I never wanted to be like——'

She broke off. She didn't want to run down her mother but, in truth, it had been very hard living with a promiscuous single parent.

'I know what you're referring to, Salome,' Mike said gently. 'I'm not blind. I can see Molly set you a rotten example. It's to your credit and yours alone that you turned out as lovely and sweet as you are. Oh, darling, you've made me so happy, knowing you never went to bed with Ralph.' His smile was wry and regretful. 'Funny, isn't it, how we human beings are so quick to judge others? I took one look at you, then at your middle-aged husband, put two and two together, and came up with five.'

'You're not the only one, Mike. Everyone thought I'd married Ralph for his money. That's why I . . . I . . .'

'You what?'

'I gave away all the money he settled on me when we separated.'

She glanced up at him, and saw he was startled, then mildly exasperated. 'You are a silly, proud, stubborn, wonderful little ninny!'

'Am I?'

'Of course you are! And what rubbish you talk sometimes! You had every right to every cent he gave you. You married him in good faith, loved him as best you could. He took the so-called best years of your life, and you had a right to—— Hey! What about this unit? And that Ferrari?' He gave her a close, wary look. 'Are you pulling my leg, Salome? You're not going to tell me you didn't take those?'

She looked sheepish. 'Originally, I was going to sell them. But then I decided to keep a little for myself, since I couldn't bear the thought of going back to live with Molly and Wayne. After that, my life changed somewhat. This sexy, handsome neighbour seduced me, and I decided to stick around for a while.'

'Did he? The cad! What did he do, pray tell? Did he by chance do this?' He bent and ran a seductive tongue-tip around her mouth. 'And perhaps this?' His hand slipped under her jumper to cover her breast. 'And this?' His thumb rubbed her nipple to instant hardness.

Salome was constantly amazed how quickly Mike could arouse her, make her forget everything but wanting him.

'Marry me,' he murmured against her mouth. 'I'll get us a special licence. We could be man and wife within a week.'

He must have felt her automatic freeze, for his hand immediately retreated, his head lifting. 'What's wrong now?' he asked, a black frown bunching his brows together. 'You said you loved me.'

'Yes, of course I love you. But to be married, within a week of Ralph's death? Mike, it...it won't look right.'

'What does it matter what it looks like?' he scowled impatiently.

'But it *does* matter,' she insisted. 'To *me*. Can't you see, Mike? I'm fed up with people looking down their noses at me, thinking I'm some sort of tramp for sale to the highest bidder. And what of your parents? They'd be horrified. It'll be bad enough their finding out I was a divorced woman, without anything else to blacken my character. If I'm to be your wife, I want their good opinion. They think I'm a good girl, and I——'

'You *are* a good girl,' Mike cut in frustratedly.

'I know that and you know that, but other people believe what they read in the newspapers.'

Mike shook his head at her with fond indulgence in his eyes. 'Tell me what you want.'

Salome levered herself upright and scrambled from his lap, curling up on the sofa next to him and taking both his hands in hers. 'I want a proper courtship, a proper engagement, a proper wedding. No rush-job.'

His expression was wryly amused. 'Do you have any idea what that will entail? I'm Italian, in case you've forgotten, with very traditional parents. Give them licence and our wedding day will rival that of Charles and Diana!'

Salome looked down. Was she being selfish, wanting her wedding to Mike to be a very special day with a church ceremony and all the trimmings? Should she give in and do what he wanted, marry in haste?

No, she decided thoughtfully. A woman had a right to have her needs and wants fulfilled as much as a man. If she gave in in this, Mike might start treating her as Ralph had done—as if she were a malleable child with no will of her own. As a mature adult, she knew her love for Mike wouldn't survive such treatment. She looked up with fresh resolve in her heart.

'Good,' she said firmly. 'That's the way it should be. When Ralph and I were married, it was a brief register office job with no real heart. We didn't even have any photographs taken. This time, I'd like to have the lot.'

'You'll get the lot all right!' Mike assured her with a dry laugh. 'And more besides, I'll warrant.'

Salome's heart squeezed tight with dismay. Surely he wasn't going to argue with her about this, was he? If he loved her as much as he said he did, couldn't he see how disastrous that would be for their future relationship? 'Please, Mike, I love you very much, and want to please you, but this is very important to me.'

He stared across at her, then smiled, one of his hands lifting gently against her cheek. 'Yes, of course it is . . . I'm just being selfish, wanting you all to myself as quickly as possible without considering what *you* want. We'll wait a respectable amount of time, announce our engagement, then bite the bullet and give our respective parents the full steam ahead sign for a church ceremony and reception. They're all sure to want a hand in it. In fact, I have a feeling that your Molly might be as bad as my mother. Never have I seen a woman so ready for romance!'

Salome grinned. 'Like mother, like daughter, wouldn't you say?' She took his hand and pressed the open palm to her mouth.

'Mm. None of that now. I have some prerequisites of my own before I'm too distracted.'

She stopped kissing his palm. 'What prerequisites?'

'First things first. What about babies?'

'What about them?'

He gave her a sardonic look. 'Married Italian men produce *bambinos*. If they don't, people start looking down their noses at them and saying unmentionable things behind their backs. You're not the only one who has feelings, you know.'

'Oh, well, in that case... Would six be enough, do you think?'

'Six?' He looked horrified. 'My God, I was thinking of one. Or maybe two.'

She grinned. 'Yes. I think two would be fine. Two of each.'

'That's *four*,' he pointed out drily.

Salome opened her eyes in mock horror. 'Good grief, the man can *count*!'

Now Mike's eyes narrowed. 'Something tells me our marriage is not going to be exactly as I imagined.'

'Oh? And how did you imagine it?'

He stood up, picked her up in his arms, and started carrying her towards the main bedroom. 'I have these visions of you, waiting every night, dressed in a slinky black négligé. Something very sheer, so I can see you've got nothing on underneath. I come in, we have a drink together, followed by a long candle-lit meal, then off to bed for some marvellously imaginative lovemaking. That is, of course, on the nights we make it that far. Sometimes, I take you to bed first and leave the drinks and meal till afterwards...'

He sighed as he reached the side of the double bed. 'Hard to do either if Junior runs in or the baby's crying.'

Salome knew Mike was only joking. He was going to make a marvellous father, proud and doting. Most likely *she* would be the one who would end up being neglected while he played with his children!

'I have another scenario,' she said with a twinkle in her eye. 'A more immediate one.'

'Sounds promising. Shoot.'

'First, you put me down on this bed...'

'Done!'

'Then you undress me...'

His eyes shot upwards, but his hands were eager to comply.

'Then you undress yourself...'

'I thought you'd never ask!'

She laughed as he tossed his clothes aside with manic haste. 'What now?' he asked eagerly.

'And now,' she whispered huskily, 'we conduct dress rehearsals for our baby-making technique, so that when the moment comes, in a couple of years, we'll do it right.'

'Did I hear correctly? You said a couple of years?' He grinned widely. 'You mean I have two times three hundred and sixty-five nights before I have to embrace fatherhood?'

'I don't believe in rushing things.'

Those beautiful black eyes travelled over her impatient flesh. 'Neither do I, darling. Neither do I...' And he slowly, ever so slowly, set about making love to her.

Hi,

Italy, as always, is
a model's paradise.
But I'm tired of the
obligatory parties,
the devouring eyes.
Particularly those
of Nicolo Sabatini,
who seems to think
I should be for his
eyes only.

Love, Caroline

HARLEQUIN®

PRESENTS: *Plus*

Meet Matt Hunter. He doesn't recognize that Nicola, his new assistant, is the woman who shared his bed one night, eight long years ago. Hardly flattering, but then Nicola has no intention of reminding him of the occasion!

And then there's Grant Goodman. He *must* know about Briony's past, but it hasn't stopped him from hiring her to manage his newest resort in Tasmania. And it may explain his sordid propositions—which Briony could easily ignore if she didn't find Grant so attractive!

Matt and Grant are just two of the sexy men you'll fall in love with each month in Harlequin Presents Plus.

Don't miss

Past Passion by Penny Jordan
Harlequin Presents Plus #1655

and

Unwilling Mistress by Lindsay Armstrong
Harlequin Presents Plus #1656

Harlequin Presents Plus
The best has just gotten better!

Available in June wherever Harlequin books are sold.

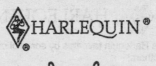

WEDDING INVITATION
Marisa Carroll

Brent Powell is marrying Jacqui Bertrand, and the whole town of Eternity is in on the plans. This is to be the first wedding orchestrated by the newly formed community co-op, Weddings, Inc., and no detail is being overlooked.

Except perhaps a couple of trivialities. The bride is no longer speaking to the groom, his mother is less than thrilled with her, and her kids want nothing to do with *him*.

WEDDING INVITATION, available in June from Superromance, is the first book in Harlequin's exciting new cross-line series, **WEDDINGS, INC.** Be sure to look for the second book, **EXPECTATIONS,** by Shannon Waverly (Harlequin Romance #3319), coming in July.

WED-1

HARLEQUIN®

Don't miss these Harlequin favorites by some of our most distinguished authors!
And now, you can receive a discount by ordering two or more titles!

HT #25551	THE OTHER WOMAN by Candace Schuler	$2.99	☐
HT #25539	FOOLS RUSH IN by Vicki Lewis Thompson	$2.99	☐
HP #11550	THE GOLDEN GREEK by Sally Wentworth	$2.89	☐
HP #11603	PAST ALL REASON by Kay Thorpe	$2.99	☐
HR #03228	MEANT FOR EACH OTHER by Rebecca Winters	$2.89	☐
HR #03268	THE BAD PENNY by Susan Fox	$2.99	☐
HS #70532	TOUCH THE DAWN by Karen Young	$3.39	☐
HS #70540	FOR THE LOVE OF IVY by Barbara Kaye	$3.39	☐
HI #22177	MINDGAME by Laura Pender	$2.79	☐
HI #22214	TO DIE FOR by M.J. Rodgers	$2.89	☐
HAR #16421	HAPPY NEW YEAR, DARLING by Margaret St. George	$3.29	☐
HAR #16507	THE UNEXPECTED GROOM by Muriel Jensen	$3.50	☐
HH #28774	SPINDRIFT by Miranda Jarrett	$3.99	☐
HH #28782	SWEET SENSATIONS by Julie Tetel	$3.99	☐

Harlequin Promotional Titles

#83259	UNTAMED MAVERICK HEARTS (Short-story collection featuring Heather Graham Pozzessere, Patricia Potter, Joan Johnston)	$4.99	☐

(limited quantities available on certain titles)

	AMOUNT	$
DEDUCT:	10% DISCOUNT FOR 2+ BOOKS	$
	POSTAGE & HANDLING	$
	($1.00 for one book, 50¢ for each additional)	
	APPLICABLE TAXES*	$ _____
	TOTAL PAYABLE	$ _____

(check or money order—please do not send cash)

To order, complete this form and send it, along with a check or money order for the total above, payable to Harlequin Books, to: **In the U.S.:** 3010 Walden Avenue, P.O. Box 9047, Buffalo, NY 14269-9047; **In Canada:** P.O. Box 613, Fort Erie, Ontario, L2A 5X3.

Name: _____

Address: _____ City: _____

State/Prov.: _____ Zip/Postal Code: _____

*New York residents remit applicable sales taxes.
 Canadian residents remit applicable GST and provincial taxes.

HBACK-AJ